Dear Rea

This is

Debutante ___ you

enjoyed reading about the lives of the McCool women.

The location for Snowy Montana Nights is Gardiner, Montana at the northern entrance to Yellowstone. Gardiner does exist. It's a lovely town where I was fortune enough to spend a couple of weeks. However, I played a little fast and loose with amenities available there, as well as available hotels. So visit the town yourself and see what I made up. I think you'll enjoy the city.

My couple visits the Old Saloon in Emigrant, Montana for dinner. The Old Saloon does exist. My husband and I had a wonderful meal there. Really a fascinating place. There was no live music while we were there, but their website has a list of live musical acts scheduled. If you are in the area, try their Cowboy Burger.

My hero's family ranch is named Grizzly Bitter-root Ranch, as suggested by Ruth Smithson of Colorado. The ranch was based (initially) on the Smith Family Ranch where I fortunate to stay in 2017. Like Pike and Coda in my story, the ranch had Border Collies, although one of them was only ten weeks old, and for those who know me, yes, I did try (unsuccess-fully!) to steal Coda (the puppy.) While I started with the Smith Family Ranch in my head, the ranch in the book comprises hundreds of acres more land. My sincere thank you and gratitude to the Smith family for their warm hospitalities and willingness to answer all my questions. Any inaccurate information about horse ranches and living and working on one is completely my error.

Thank you for staying with me.

Cynthia D'Alba

SNOWY MONTANA NIGHTS

Dallas Debutantes/McCool Trilogy (Book 3)

CYNTHIA D'ALBA

Praise for Cynthia D'Alba

An emotional, complex and beautiful story of love and life and how it can all change in a heartbeat.

—DiDi, Guilty Pleasures Book Reviews on *Texas Lullaby*

Highly recommend to all fans of hot cowboys, firefighters, and romance.

—Emily, Goodreads on *Saddles and Soot*

This author does an amazing job of keeping readers on their toes while maintaining a natural flow to the story.

—RT Book Reviews on *Texas Hustle*

Cynthia D'Alba's *Texas Fandango* from Samhain lets readers enjoy the sensual fun in the sun […] This latest offering gives readers a sexy escape and a reason to seek out D'Alba's earlier titles.

—Library Journal Reviews on *Texas Fandango*

[…] inclusions that stand out for all the right reasons is Cynthia D'Alba's clever *Backstage Pass*

—Publisher's Weekly on *Backstage Pass* in *Cowboy Heat*

Texas Two Step kept me on an emotional roller coaster […] an emotionally charged romance, with well-developed characters and an engaging secondary cast. A quarter of the way into the book I added Ms. D'Alba to my auto-buys.

—5 Stars and Recommended Read, Guilty Pleasure Book Reviews on *Texas Two Step*

[..]Loved this book…characters came alive. They had depth, interest and completeness. But more than the romance and sex which were great, there are connections with family and friends which makes this story so much more than a story about two people.

—Night Owl Romance 5 STARS! A TOP PICK *on Texas Bossa Nova*

Wow, what an amazing romance novel. *Texas Lullaby* is an impassioned, well-written book with a genuine love story that took hold of my heart and soul from the very beginning.

—LJT, Amazon Reviews, on *Texas Lullaby*

Texas Lullaby is a refreshing departure from the traditional romance plot in that it features an already committed couple.

—Tangled Hearts Book Reviews on *Texas Lullaby*

[…]sexy, contemporary western has it all. Scorching sex, a loving family and suspenseful danger. Oh, yeah!

—Bookaholics Romance Book Club on *Texas Hustle*

Also by Cynthia D'Alba

Brotherhood Protectors

(Part of Elle James Brotherhood Series)

Texas Ranger Rescue

Texas Marine Mayhem

Copyright

Cover Artist: Elle James

Editor: Heidi Shaham

To Dr. Issam Makhoul (in my southern accent, it sounds like "McCool") Without, I wouldn't exists and neither would this book.

For my street team: D'Alba Diamonds. You've stood behind me even when I couldn't write. You supported me and gave me excellent advice, sometimes when I asked and sometimes when I didn't. Never stop. You make me a better writer.

Chapter One

❧❧❧

W endy McCool watched her cousin Mae walk
down the aisle toward her groom, her face
radiant with happiness. Roy, her groom, had a line of
sweat across his brow. Of course, from what Wendy
had observed in the many—too many—weddings
she'd served as a bridesmaid, most guys standing at
the altar of marriage had a little sweat going on.

At this wedding, Wendy was more than just the
maid of honor. She'd been the one to introduce Mae
to Roy. Wendy had been seeing Roy's older brother.
However, they'd never been more than convenient
plus ones to events that required not showing up
alone. It'd worked well for them.

But Roy and Mae had taken a different path,
falling in love and now getting married.

Wendy was thrilled for Mae, and for Roy of
course. Heavens knew, she'd done all she could to help
this day happen. With Roy's older brother as best man

and him having a job that took him out of town for days or weeks at a time, Wendy had stepped in to do not only her own maid-of-honor duties, but all of the best man's too. She didn't mind. Anything for family. And, to be brutally honest, although she worked long hours as a surgeon, the wedding had been a welcome distraction from the ennui she'd been feeling.

The bride reached the front and Uncle Gordon took his seat beside Aunt Alice. Mae turned to Wendy and passed off her bridal bouquet. Wendy smiled and gave her a way -to-go wink. Mae grinned and returned the wink.

Now that Wendy held her bouquet and the bride's bouquet in her hands, her only last maid of honor duty was to hand over the wedding ring, which she'd worn on her thumb to not lose it. She let her mind drift a little. She'd been a bridesmaid so many times, she could probably quote the preacher's words without giving it much thought.

The preacher was droning on when out of nowhere, Roy spoke. "I can't do this. I'm sorry, Mae."

Wendy startled. It wasn't time for Roy to say anything. Behind her, Wendy's twin sister and matron of honor gasped.

The bride's back straightened. "I don't understand. What's going on, Roy?"

Wendy leaned around her cousin and saw the sheen of sweat on Roy's face.

"I'm so sorry," he said. "Really, I am, but…" His gaze rolled from his bride to her attendants, and then he looked at Mae again. "I've fallen in love with someone else."

Wendy gasped, along with the five-hundred plus attendees sitting in the church pews. The microphone that'd been placed at the front of the church to ensure their vows could be heard throughout the massive chapel now broadcast everything Roy and Mae said. Their words reached every corner of the cathedral and every gossip's ear.

"I'm sorry, you did what?" Mae yelled at him. "Who? When? Where? How?"

The "how" reverberated over the audience's murmurings.

Wendy thought about passing the bridal bouquet back to Mae so she could beat Roy over his thick skull. Mae was the best thing that'd ever happened to him. What was he thinking?

"I'm sorry," he repeated. "I can't ignore what I feel, what I know she feels, too. We would never hurt you, but when love is this strong, we can't pretend it doesn't exist."

"What the hell is he talking about?" Risa, Wendy's twin sister, whispered. "Do you have any idea what's going on?"

"Not a clue," Wendy said over her shoulder.

Roy stepped away from Mae, his face flushed and glistening with perspiration. Stepping past Mae, he walked up to Wendy and announced in a dramatic voice, "I love you. I love you with all my heart and soul. I can't stop thinking about you, dreaming about you." He reached for Wendy's hand. "I know you feel it, too."

"What?" Wendy screeched and jerked her hand back. "What are you talking about?"

The bride had whipped around in her long gown to watch where Roy was headed. Now, her brow furrowed in confusion. "Yeah, Roy. What the hell are you talking about?"

The scene playing out at the front of the church enthralled the wedding audience. There were more gasps and titters as whispering echoed in the chamber.

Wendy saw her Uncle Gordon, Mae's dad, stand. She worried there was going to be bloodshed and soon, not that she would do anything to stop him. But Roy appeared undaunted by the crowd or the uproar around him.

"Us. You and me. Together," Roy said, his expression beseeching, his hands clasped over his chest. "I love you with all my heart."

He again reached for Wendy's hand.

She again jerked it back, only with more force this time. Her startled and appalled gaze met the bride's and she shrugged with an I-have-no-idea-what's-going-on-either expression.

She glared at the groom. "Roy. I don't know what's going on in your pea brain, but I think we need to clear something up."

Wendy handed off the two bouquets to her sister, who took them, and along with hers, propped all three on her very pregnant belly. Then Wendy grabbed his arm and pulled him across the church sanctuary and through an exit door.

"Roy Livingston. What in the world are you doing? Have you lost your ever-loving, pea-picking mind?"

"I love you, Wendy." He pressed his hands over his heart. "In here, I know you love me, too."

The church door slammed open and the bride and best man charged through.

Wendy looked at her cousin and then back at Roy. "Roy. You don't love me. I don't love you. I love my cousin, Mae. Everything I did to help you was for her, not as some excuse to spend time with you."

"You can't mean that. You made sure I was always on your dates with my brother. You took me to your hair stylist," Roy said. "You kissed me."

Mae stumbled backward as she said, "You kissed him?"

"You kissed my brother?" Everett said at the same time.

Wendy blew out a breath. "*On the cheek.* Everyone calm down. I didn't *kiss* kiss him. I bussed his cheek during the tux fitting."

She stepped over to Mae and took her hand. "I would never *ever* do anything that would hurt you. Ever. With Everett's job taking him away so much, I wanted you and Roy to have the fantasy wedding, including a bachelor party for him. I tried to make everything perfect." She squeezed Mae's fingers and then turned her face to glare at Roy. "You are an idiot.

To have cold feet is one thing, but to embarrass our families like you did today is unforgivable."

Everett opened his mouth to speak and Wendy wondered if he was preparing to defend his younger brother. If he did, she might have to knee him in the groin. Now that she thought about it, that's probably what she or Mae should do to Roy. In the end, Everett shook his head and didn't say anything.

"What do you want to do, Mae?" Wendy asked. "I'm sure Risa has held off our families as long as she can."

Mae shook her head as she drew in a deep breath. "I want Roy to leave. Now."

"Then that's what will happen," Wendy said. She pointed to a gate in the wall. "The exit is that way."

Roy's shoulders sagged. He gave Wendy a sad, defeated expression, but she felt nothing but fury at his audacity of destroying her cousin. Lucky to be getting out of here with his manhood intact, he should probably hit that gate and keep on running before Uncle Gordon got hold of him.

"Come on, Roy," Everett said with a deep sigh and grabbed his brother by his shoulder.

Wendy's heart ached for Mae. This was every bride's nightmare. She thought about what she could do to help, and even though it wasn't much, she said, "I can go in and tell everyone the wedding is off if you want me to."

Mae had shut her eyes as Roy walked away. Now, she looked at Wendy, the McCool determination and fire in her eyes. "No. They were here at my invitation.

I'll go send them home, and then I need some time alone to think."

Wendy stood just inside the chapel door with Risa and watched the bravest woman she'd ever known announce the groom had left and there'd be no wedding.

That evening, Wendy knocked on Risa's condo door and let herself in. "Hey! Anyone home?"

"In the kitchen," her sister shouted back. "Help me. He's a crazy man."

Wendy laughed and headed through the condo to find her brother-in-law backing his wife into a corner. "You two knock it off," she said. "Haven't you done enough?" She gestured to Risa's protruding belly.

"Hey, sis-in-law. Get over here." Trevor wiggled his fingers and took a step toward her.

"Hell, no," Wendy said and raced around the bar to keep the obstacle between Trevor and her. "I hate to be tickled."

A laughing Risa pushed at her husband. "You are disgusting. Get out of here. Go. Wendy and I have some serious gossiping to do while dinner finishes cooking."

Trevor grabbed his wife and kissed her loudly. "What will I do without you?"

Still laughing, she pushed her husband out of the kitchen toward the den. "Watch TV. Call a friend. Just get. We've got to rehash today's non-wedding."

"Wow," said Trevor with arched eyebrows. "What a shit show." He looked at Wendy. "Sorry. That must have been awful for you." He reached for his sister-in-law, pulled her in for a hug and kissed the side of her head. "That totally sucked."

She adored Trevor. When Risa and he finally got back together, Risa's whole world changed. Wendy had never seen any two people more in love and committed. And she couldn't wait to welcome their son into the world.

"Oh," Risa said, and hugged her belly.

"You okay, honey?" Trevor asked, hurrying back to his wife's side.

"Yes," she said with an exasperated sigh. "Your son is playing soccer again in there."

Shaking his finger at Risa's belly, he said, "I warned him about that. He's grounded for at least a year." He hugged his wife and gave her a soft kiss.

"You two are totally nauseating," Wendy said. "Get a room."

Trevor looked over his shoulder, still holding onto his wife. "We have a room. You're the one keeping us from it."

Risa patted his back. "Go watch the news. We'll eat in about twenty minutes."

After another quick kiss, Trevor wandered out to the den and flipped on a local Dallas channel.

"It's disgusting how happy you are," Wendy teased.

"I know." Risa grinned and danced a little. "Who'd have thought a year ago I'd be here? I can't help that I just love him so much."

Wendy pretended to put her finger down her throat.

"So, did you talk to Mom and Dad?" Wendy asked after both of them stopped laughing.

"Mom, but just briefly. Aunt Alice is crushed for Mae and furious at Rob. Uncle Gordon's talking about finding a hit man. I'm sure he's kidding, right?" She rubbed her protruding belly while she shook her head. "Did you ever imagine something like today's craziness could happen?"

"Which?" Wendy asked, her top lip curled into a snarl. "Being left at the altar or having the whole world listen in while the groom dumps his bride for you?"

"Gosh, hard choice. I'll choose none of the above."

Wendy snorted. "Yeah, me, too, if I'd had the choice. I hope Aunt Alice and Uncle Gordon know I would never do anything that would hurt Mae. I mean, Rob? No way."

"They know. Mom said they weren't upset with you at all. That's when the mention of a hit man came up."

"I might contribute to his fee," she said with a sigh and a headshake. "Absolutely the worst nightmare, but at least it's over. Poor Mae. You know her. She'll throw herself into her job."

"What about you and Everett?"

"There never was anything between us other than convenient plus ones."

Risa frowned. "I thought you guys were a thing."

With a shrug, Wendy said, "Not really. I mean, he

looks good on my arm and we photograph well for the society pages, but beyond that, nope."

"Hey," Trevor yelled from the den. "You two need to get in here. Right now!"

The twins hurried from the kitchen—hurried being truer for Wendy than Risa, who shuffled behind as fast as a pregnant woman near term can.

"What?" Wendy asked.

Trevor pointed to the television screen.

A red-headed woman stood outside the Greater Dallas United Methodist Church and was saying, "This was the scene of a wedding that had quite the dramatic ending today when the groom announced his love for the maid of honor. Viewer Vicki Wise provided us with this video from inside the church."

There was a slight pause before a grainy video played. Because of the excellent audio system Wendy had put into place for Mae's vows, Roy's declaration of love was loud and clear, even if the picture itself lack definition.

Wendy groaned as she watched Roy trying to take her hand and her jerking it away. She said a few cuss words as she saw herself pull Roy across the chapel and out a door.

At this point, the view changed back to the news reporter. "We don't know what happened between the groom and the maid of honor, who happens to be the bride's cousin and there's been no comment from the bride's or groom's families. This is Rachel Wood reporting from Greater Dallas Methodist Church."

"Wow, Rachel. That's a crazy story," the news anchor said. "Now on to sports."

Trevor muted the television. "What are you going to do?"

Wendy shrugged. "What can I do? Nothing happened between Roy and me, and if I start giving statements and denials, then I'm outed as the maid of honor. At this point, no names have been used." She groaned and raked her hair out of her eyes. "Dammit. I could just kill Roy."

Risa put her arm around Wendy's waist. "This will pass. It's just a gossip news filler. By tomorrow, someone famous will do something and that'll become the hot item." She squeezed Wendy. "Besides, you're lucky you live here. No one will get past the security guards downstairs."

Risa and Wendy occupied the top floor of a high-rise-mid-town Dallas condominium building. Each woman had her own large three-bedroom unit with balconies that had million-dollar views of downtown Dallas. In addition, the two units shared a common garden slash patio space that had a small private pool. The units had been a surprise birthday gift from their parents. Wendy loved all the conveniences, like valet parking and concierge services. Nothing like coming home and having someone park your car for you and finding your kitchen has been totally restocked.

The building security was top-notch. Risa's husband owned Eye-Spy International, a global security company based in Texas. His first priority was ensuring the safety of his wife, son-to-be, and sister-in-law. Since he'd approved the building security, Wendy had no concerns about uninvited visitors.

"At this point, I'm not worried about the press, but you know it's only a matter of time before all the involved parties will be named." She blew out a long sigh. "I worry how my partners will take this."

Wendy was a medical partner in the largest, and most respected, plastic surgery practices in Dallas. But rumors that she'd slept with her cousin's fiancé or had done anything unethical to lure him away from her cousin could adversely affect the referrals. Who wanted a homewrecker as their doctor? Frankly, excellent plastic surgeons were plentiful in Dallas and she could be replaced. That hard reality often had her questioning her medical specialty choice.

Risa patted her shoulder. "Honestly, this will be old news by Monday. Mark my word."

The story did die down after a while, but not before an enterprising reporter at Dallas Star News reran the wedding story complete with the names of all parties involved. Finally, the wedding tale faded from public attention when the quarterback of the Dallas Panthers ran his million-dollar Ferrari into the backend of a parked Dallas SWAT truck, giving the gossips new grist for their rumor mills.

Even when her fifteen-minutes of notoriety had faded, Wendy still felt off, itchy, like she needed to make some changes.

She was proud of the medical career she'd built. She took great pride in helping patients who needed her skills to resume their lives. Lately, however, she'd performed so many eyelifts, rhinoplasties, liposuctions, and facelifts that she'd begun to question if this was what she'd spent years and years of schooling and hours and hours of study to do with her life. A restless energy thrummed through her. A caged tiger had more patience than she, but she worked hard to hide her frustrations.

Even delivering her new nephew couldn't pull her from her funk. Risa's obstetrician had been in the delivery room, but her sister had asked Wendy to be the one who welcomed her son into the world.

When Wendy held the newborn in her gloved hands, little Stephen Samuel Mason held Wendy's heart in his tiny hands. She couldn't get enough of him. Her nephew brought a new light into her life. She worshiped him. Other than her sister, she'd never loved anyone with such deep feelings, but even he wasn't enough to stem her restlessness.

In fact, she was a little embarrassed at how much she envied her sister right now. Risa was so in love with her husband and her baby that Wendy's melancholy with her own life came to a new high.

Oh, she didn't want a baby of her own right now, but she desperately wanted her sister's level of joy. Wendy needed to believe that she was in the right place and doing what she was meant to do with her life.

She was a doctor, for goodness sake. She'd spent countless years and energy getting to where she was. She'd dedicated every free minute to building her practice and her reputation, even to the exclusion of any serious personal relationships. She made the decision to do this with her life, so now it was irrational that she would be discontented. One thing was certain. She needed a change, something that would shake up her life.

The only problem was, she had no idea what action to take. She only knew whatever she did would require her taking a leap of faith off a cliff, one that included a leave from her practice and a temporary relocation from the safety net of her Texas family. She needed to go somewhere and get her head together, discover if she was on the right path for her or if there was something better waiting around the corner.

For the first time in her life, she would be living away from her twin. It was like amputating a part of herself and leaving it behind.

She was terrified.

Chapter Two

❧

Zane Miller clicked his tongue and squeezed his legs. The horse under him picked up her pace from barely moving to a trot. He knew that's all he'd get today from this mare, and that was fine. This was only a bit of exercise for Belle. The mare's owner lived out of state in the winter and boarded the mare at Grizzly Bitterroot Ranch during those months. Not all Montana horse ranches would take on boarding in the winter for absentee owners. Winter time boarding meant additional staffing, but for the Miller ranch, the extra winter fees came in handy. One thing was for sure—no one got rich going into the horse-boarding business.

Grizzly Bitterroot had been started by Zane's grandfather and was still owned by his parents. However, after his mother's illness last year, his parents had headed off to Florida for winter sunshine and no snow, leaving Zane—who'd only been back in Montana for six months—in charge.

The cell phone on his belt vibrated. Zane slowed Belle to a walk and pulled his phone out. His mother.

"Hey, Mom," he said as a way of greeting. "How's Florida?"

"Eighties with bright sun."

Zane looked up at the gray sky that promised more snow later. "Rub it in, why don't you?" he said jokingly.

As he hoped, she laughed. "How are things there?"

"Good. Cowboy Russ and I have it under control. I'm out on Misty Simpson's horse this morning."

"She's a sweet gal. Very calm."

"The owner or the horse?" he joked.

His mom laughed again. "The horse."

"Belle'd be perfect for some beginner riding lessons in the spring."

"Talk to Misty. She would probably be glad to loan you Belle for that. Since the birth of her twins, her time is quite limited."

"Uh-huh," he said, distracted by a moose and calf walking across the pasture in the distance.

He lifted his binoculars to watch the moose amble along. Sure, he'd seen lots of moose growing up here, but he'd lived away so long that seeing all the wildlife again made his return to Montana worth it. Chicago had its perks, but the wildlife, this view, and the clean air certainly weren't any of them.

His mother began talking about her college days

and sorority sisters she was still in contact with and something about a wedding and a jilted bride.

He mumbled "Uh-huh" a couple of times so his mother would think he was listening, but when she got going, his eyes had a tendency to glaze over.

"So I told Janet we would be happy to have Wendy stay at the ranch for a while. That won't be a problem, will it?"

He caught her last sentence and startled. Lowering the field glasses, he said, "Wait. What? You're sending someone to the ranch?"

She sighed. "Sometimes, you don't hear a word I say. You're just like your father. Yes, my friend Janet has a daughter who needs a break from her life in Dallas. I said our little ranch is a perfect place for her to R&R."

"Our ranch?" he repeated. "In the middle of winter. It's December, Mom."

"I know what month it is, but she can stay in the barn apartment. It's tiny, but she'd have all the privacy she needs."

"What am I supposed to do with her?"

"Just treat her nicely. She's had a couple of rough months."

Ah. The pieces connected in his head. This is the jilted bride from the epic saga his mother had been regaling him with earlier.

He released a silent groan. Great. Just great. That's all he needed. Another mouth to feed in between her wailing and crying over some guy.

"Has she ever been on a ranch? Know anything about horses?"

"Oh, honey, I don't know for sure, but I think so. Janet inherited her family's ranch, so I assume her daughter rides, but we didn't talk about that. Poor Janet was just so beside herself about that whole wedding disaster that I wanted to do whatever I could to help."

"That's fine. I'll take care of it."

Mentally, he moved repairing the barn apartment to the top of his list. He hadn't mentioned anything to his parents, but the hot water tank had finally given out, dropping its entire one-hundred-gallon load and flooding the downstairs. Of course, the temperature had bottomed out that night and everything had frozen. He, Cowboy Russ and Russ's wife Lori had chipped the ice and mopped up the melted mess, but the flooring and baseboards would have to be replaced. And he might have to replace the sofa before the apartment would be suitable for a guest.

Being that today was early December, she'd probably come right after Christmas, which gave him three weeks to get it all done. It'd be close, but he'd make it work. He'd do anything to make his mom happy.

"I knew you would, honey," his mom said. "Now, she'll be there this afternoon about four."

"Be where?" he asked, hoping like hell she didn't mean what he feared she meant.

"Gardiner. She's flying into the Gardiner airport. I told her you'd pick her up. Give her the keys to my

SUV to drive while she's there. No sense in her renting something when my old car needs to be driven."

His mom's "old car" was a two-year old Jeep Grand Cherokee without a scratch on it.

His heart sank to his knees. Crap and double crap.

"Honey, you still there?" his mother said. "Did I lose you?"

"No, no. I'm here. I'm out on Ridgeback trail and the phone service fades in and out. You know that."

"So four o'clock. You'll pick her up?"

"I'll pick her up," he said somewhat grudgingly. "What's her name?"

His mother chuckled. "Yes, I suppose you would need to know that. Wendy McCool."

"Got it. Wendy McCool. Four today."

"Thanks, sweetheart. Love you."

"Love you too, Mom."

In general, he kept his parents fully informed with ranch decisions he'd made or problems he'd come across. The water damage in the apartment was the exception. The problems thus far had been so minor as to be insignificant. However, a major issue like needing to rebuild some of the guest quarters and replacing the furniture would have brought them back to Montana posthaste and that's the last thing he wanted. After battling cancer for two years, his mother deserved this Florida winter vacation and he was determined she get it.

Besides, he had plans for that barn apartment, a major overhaul that he hadn't mentioned to his folks yet. Plans that included adding a thousand square feet and making the space into a temporary home for him. In fact, he'd already begun drawing up plans for what he wanted to build come spring. After living in Chicago for the past twenty years, he was home in Montana for good and he needed somewhere to live other than his old bedroom, not that the expanded apartment would be permanent for him either. By the time his brother Eli returned from service, Zane planned to have finished building his dream house on land a few miles up the road.

The water damage had been unfortunate, but ripping out the floors and tearing down the walls were steps one and two of his renovation plan, so he hadn't lost much sleep over the dead water tank and extensive water damage. Who would've thought he'd have company in the middle of winter?

Belle wasn't thrilled when he goosed her into a steady trot back to the ranch, but he promised her an extra scoop of oats once they got there. The mare must have understood his oat promise, because she headed for the barn at a quicker pace than she'd offered that entire ride.

There was no time to clean up before he left for the airport. He did do a quick onceover of the main house and assured himself everything was at least acceptable.

Luckily for him, Russ and his wife lived in a small apartment adjacent to the main barn. Lori tackled the dust and dirt in the main house on a weekly basis, which was all he wanted or needed. After a day on the ranch, the last thing he wanted to do was mop or vacuum. Of course, the same had been true when he lived in Chicago as a hedge fund manager, only he'd had a woman who'd come in three times a week to clean, grocery shop, and maintain his wardrobe.

He was fortunate Lori had been there just this morning. Everything was in its place and no dirty dishes littered the kitchen counter.

Once downstairs met his approval, he jogged up the stairs to check his brother's old room. Since Zane lived alone in the main house and wasn't using Eli's room for anything, Lori could have skipped cleaning it, but the room smelled of furniture polish and fresh linens. It would have to do, unless she wanted to take his parents' master bedroom. That'd be fine with him, too. He sure didn't want it.

A little before four, he pulled onto the gravel drive that led to the small public airport. There was only one runway, so he couldn't miss the small, private jet as it settled on the rough gravel and tar airstrip. At this time of year, the little airport didn't get much use, but during the summer months, there were usually a number of planes using it for various tourist activities such as skydiving.

The plane rolled to a stop and then taxied back to the main area where he was parked. Snow, in the form of fat, wet flakes landed with heavy splats on his windshield as he waited with dread. A rich girl wanting to play cowgirl. Not what he needed right now.

In a minute, a door on the jet opened and a set a stairs were lowered. A man wearing a pilot's uniform exited and stopped at the base of the steps. He extended his hand and assisted a tall, blonde woman down.

Zane's gaze slid along a pair of lightweight linen pants covering long, shapely legs that seemed to go on forever. A simple white blouse and blazer accented her generous breasts and narrow shoulders. Sunglasses, completely unnecessary at this time of day in this weather, covered not only her eyes, but a major portion of her face. Still, he could see a sharp nose and a high brow. He was amazed she hadn't broken her neck walking down the steep steps in a pair of high heeled shoes better suited for the boardroom than Montana in December.

As she removed her sunglasses and looked around at the scenery surrounding the private airstrip, fluffy snowflakes quickly dotted her shoulders and hair.

Zane snorted and shook his head. She wouldn't last a week at the ranch, which was too bad. She was a serious contender for the most beautiful woman he'd ever seen, and he'd seen plenty in his Chicago days, including Priscilla Roth, his ex-fiancée. After barely escaping with his balls intact from that disaster, he lacked any enthusiasm for another relationship. Maybe in six months or so, but not now, which was tragic. This Wendy chick had simply landed in his life at the wrong time.

He started his truck and drove to where she stood.

"You must be Wendy McCool," he said as he slid from the driver's seat.

She nodded. "I am." Her gaze took him in, his old and very dirty truck, and the barely there runway, and then dismissed what she saw with a wave of her hand. "This is Gardiner?"

"Yes, ma'am. You might want to get in my truck. I left the heater running."

"You're Zane Miller?"

He grinned. "Only for the last thirty-eight years or so. I hope you've got a warm coat in one of those." He gestured to the four large suitcases the pilot had pulled from the plane's underbelly.

Four huge cases. Had she brought everything she owned with her?

She rubbed her arms. "Yeah. I should have carried it on, I guess, but it was close to fifty when I flew out of Dallas and I hate to keep up with a coat. I knew the plane would be warm enough that I wouldn't need it on there. Guess I wasn't thinking about this end of the flight. What a goose, right?"

"Uh-huh," he said, absentmindedly as he hefted one of the suitcases and almost staggered. He wasn't a weak man by anyone's standards. Every day, he moved at least a few hundred-pound hay bales, but this piece of luggage had caught him off guard. He'd expected fifty pounds or something in that area. This baby had to weigh at least seventy-five pounds.

"What have you got in here?" he asked as he chucked the fancy luggage into the back of his truck. "Rocks?"

"If that's the heavy one, shoes."

He looked at her with astonishment. "You have an entire suitcase of shoes?"

She shrugged and wrinkled her nose. "I wasn't

sure what I would need, so…" She smiled. "I might have brought everything."

Pretty much what he'd assumed. "We do have stores in Montana, you know."

"I think I've heard that."

After the four cases were in the truck bed, Wendy turned to the pilot. "Thank you for getting me here, Red."

"When you get ready to come home, just let your daddy know and I'll come get you."

She hugged the older man. "Thank you."

"You take care."

The pilot tipped his head toward Zane and climbed back into the plane.

Zane and Wendy settled into the warm interior of the truck and watched as the plane taxied and lifted into the sky.

As he pulled out of the airport and turned left onto Highway 89, he asked, "Have a good flight?"

"Okay. Nothing special."

Right. Nothing special about arriving by private jet when you're the only passenger.

"So how far to your family's ranch?" she asked.

He glanced over. She was staring straight ahead. He wasn't sure if she was concerned about his driving, his driving in snow, or the distance they had to travel in the furious snow storm. The weather had definitely taken a turn for the worse in the past hour.

"Not far. Twenty miles or so."

He looked at her again and saw her well-mani-cured fingers knotted together in her lap.

"Nervous about my driving?"

She gave him a quick glance and then turned back to the road. "We don't get a lot of snow in Dallas, and when we do, the roads become Mad Max and the Thunderdome."

He laughed. The lady had a sense of humor. "Round here, the biggest risk is deer and elk crossing the road. Most of the drivers are locals and have been dealing with Montana winter weather for years."

She nodded. "Thank you again for picking me up. I really owe your mom for giving me a place to, um, think."

"Right. My parents. Well, there's some good news and some bad news. Which do you want first?"

Chapter Three

✦❧✦

Wendy laced and twisted her fingers in her lap. First, she was cold. The truck's heater was blasting on full, but she'd gotten wet standing in the snow while Red had singlehandedly unloaded the plane. Oscar, the co-pilot, had stayed in the cockpit filing their return flight route.

Second, she'd dressed all wrong. Thinking her mother's friend would be picking her up, she'd wanted to make a good first impression and worn a classic outfit. However, instead of impressing anyone, she looked like an idiot for not wearing her heavy coat. Of course, she'd known it would be cold in Montana, but in her defense, she'd thought the Gardiner Airport would have at least a single terminal. She'd envisioned simply running from the plane to the terminal and then to a car waiting close by. She hadn't envisioned standing in heavy snow.

And lastly, she was nervous. She didn't know this

man or these people. Maybe, as her sister had suggested, she had lost her freaking mind. Leaving her medical practice and going off to the middle of nowhere Montana in December did sound a little irrational even to her. All she knew was that she had to get out of town and think.

Maybe Risa had been right, and she should have gone to a Caribbean island for sun. But Wendy had wanted to go somewhere she'd never been, where she had no memories to drag up when she was supposed to be doing some heavy thinking. At the time her mother had mentioned her friend's horse ranch, it'd sounded like the perfect solution. Wendy loved horses and missed her family home. Plus, she'd never been to Montana and her mother's friend had been so convincing that this was the perfect place for Wendy to get some peace and quiet.

Now that she studied the snow collecting on the windshield, road, and piles on the road shoulders, she wondered just how clearly she'd been thinking when she agreed to this. But she was here now and she'd make the best of it. Besides, she loved using her aunt and uncle's condo in Colorado for skiing, and this adventure would be like that only with horses, right?

She tried to subtly study the man beside her. Tall with dark hair that had a few silver highlights on the side and a serious brooding expression, he looked the stereotypic cowboy with jeans splotched with dirt and something she hoped wasn't manure. His muddy boots had seen better days. His hair was at least three weeks past needing a cut and his face stubble suggested he'd missed a razor for more than a couple of days. Even with all those negatives—if the curl of his brown and silver hair over his collar and the sexy scruff could be considered negatives—the man was a walking, talking hunk.

Testosterone and pheromones oozed from every pore and she could barely stifle the shiver that ran down her spine with every inhale. She would place a hefty bet that the ranch would be a popular place for single ladies come spring. Her mother had mentioned the ranch pulled in a lot of visitors in the summer. He had to be one of the big draws for Grizzly Bitterroot Ranch.

Heck, maybe the local gals took advantage of the snowy Montana weather that kept vacationers away and made their moves on him while they had this delicious man all to themselves during the winter months. That'd be her plan of attack if she lived here, not that she had—nor needed—a plan of attack. Right now, she had absolutely no interest in starting any type of involvement with any man. The ladies could fight among themselves for his attention.

The wipers swished back and forth, removing another layer of snow.

"Don't you want to know the good news and bad news?" he asked with a smile she bet melted even the most frozen heart.

Lucky for her, her heart wasn't frozen. It was simply dead.

"Sure. Bring it on. After this fall, I can take anything."

He tossed a frown her way. "I'm not sure I know what you mean."

She waved him off. "Ignore me. I'm being pissy. What do I need to know?"

He turned off the highway onto a paved road that ended after a couple of hundred feet. They rattled across an old-fashioned covered bridge and turned left again.

"Did your mother happen to mention that my mother has been ill?"

Wendy's mouth dropped. "No. I am so sorry. I don't want to be an imposition on her."

"You won't be. Dad took Mom to Florida for the winter. I'm running the ranch while they're gone."

"So—" she swallowed hard, "—it's just the two of us at the ranch?" She thought about the private apartment her mother had assured her she would have at her disposal.

With a chuckle, he said, "Don't panic. There are other people there. Cowboy Russ and his wife Lori live in an apartment on the property. Plus, we have cowboys who come when we need a hand and many of the horses' owners are there multiple times a week. So, you aren't exactly stranded all alone with a strange man."

"Whew," she said, running the back of her hand across her forehead as though removing sweat. The truth was, after Roy had so badly misinterpreted her actions, she wasn't sure she wanted to be alone with a man for a while.

"But," he continued, "the bad news is that the hot-water tank in the apartment went out last month."

"Yikes."

"Yikes is right. The downstairs flooded, froze, and then melted the next day. We got all the water out, but not before there was significant damage to the floors and walls. I haven't gotten around to working on it, nor looking for furniture to replace the ruined stuff. So, unfortunately, the apartment isn't fit to live in right now."

As he was speaking, he turned onto another dirt road and followed it about a mile before driving between two rock and concrete entrance posts and down a long drive that separated two fenced pastures.

"Oh dear. I gather you haven't told your parents?"

"Nope. I want them to have a wonderful winter vacation and not worry about the place. Not like they could do anything about it that I can't. So, I'm sorry, but there's no apartment."

She shut her eyes and dropped her head back on the seat with a long, loud sigh. "This just isn't my year. Is there a hotel you can take me to?"

"You don't need to do that. There's plenty of room at the main ranch house. You can stay in my brother's room."

"Oh, no, Zane. I can't put you and your brother out like that."

"My brother, Eli, is stationed in Iraq, so he won't be needing his room. And it's no imposition. The room's just sitting there empty. Besides…" He glanced over and gave her a warm smile. "I can't wait to tell him there's a beautiful woman sleeping in his bed."

She knew he meant the words to be flattering, but right now, the last thing she wanted was another man who could misinterpret a situation.

"I'm at a loss for words. You are so kind to offer me your brother's room, but I don't feel at all comfortable putting you out like that. Maybe after I've had a good night's sleep, I can come up with a better plan."

He pulled to a stop in front of a two-story, log house with a wide porch that ran the entire width of the front. Fingers of dead grass poked through the snow filling an area that she supposed defined the front yard. Dead stalks from summer flowers stood like tiny posts, collecting the snow as it filled their beds. Just past the house, she could see a small copse of trees inside a fence that was topped with wire. A sign on the fence gate read, "Warning. Electricity in Use."

She pointed to the trees. "Why do you have trees fenced in?"

"Those are my mom's apple and pear trees. The bears love them and will pick them clean without a little zap as an incentive to move on down the road." He chuckled. "You should have seen how mad my mother was the year the bears ate every one of her apples. She put up the fence, and they just climbed over it and made themselves at home. It took the electrified wire to discourage them."

Her eyes were wide. "Bears? Now?"

With a grin, he said, "No, not now. It's December.

They're all resting up for spring. What do they teach you ladies down there in Texas?"

Laughing, she replied, "I knew that. I was just pulling your chain."

He chuckled. "Right now, no electricity on the fence. Come spring, believe me, it'll be fired up at the first bear sighting."

She wouldn't be here in the spring, so bears weren't something she had to worry about.

"Come on in. Let's get you settled," he said as he opened the driver's door.

"Okay," she said over the truck's roof after she'd gotten out. "But just for tonight. I'll call around tomorrow for a hotel or somewhere else I can move."

He hoisted two of the suitcases out of the truck bed. "I'll take these up and come back for the others."

"I can help," she protested. "I carried them down from my condo to the elevator." She lifted one of the bags out and set it on the ground. "Wow. I think I might have overpacked."

He was laughing as he walked by her toward the house. "Did you leave any clothes at home?"

She thought about her twelve-by-twelve walk-in closet. She'd barely made a dent.

"A few things," she said, pulling the second case from the truck. Grabbing the handles on the luggage, she began pulling them toward the house. Unfortunately, the parking area was gravel so the wheels skid in the snow and pebbles, leaving long gouges as she tugged.

After Zane set his two pieces on the front porch,

he hurried back and took the two she was wrestling with.

"Let me," he said, and picked up each piece as though they only weighed ten pounds each.

She followed him up the porch steps. Once there, she stopped and turned around to study the view. The ranch had an ideal location along a rambling river that ran along all the acreage. A fenced paddock stood directly in front of the house with only a single-lane dirt road separating them. The road led to pastures farther away. They had passed a large, red barn on their drive in. It now stood off to her left. Directly beside the house was a garage, or maybe it was another barn. She couldn't tell. There was a bob truck parked in front of the double doors of that building. Beyond the dirt road they'd come in on, another road led up and around hills and more pastures.

"This is beautiful," she said, gesturing to the view.

"Thanks. I agree. My great-grandparents were lucky to grab all this land. At today's prices, we could never afford to own all this. Back in the early nineteen-thirties, my grandparents sold off some of the farthest land from the main ranch. It was rocky and not good grazing land at all."

"What is it now?"

"Fed land. Federal national park with tent camping and hiking trails."

"Does it get used much?"

"Nope. We use some of the trails in the spring and summer for horse rides, but we rarely see people there.

When we do, they are the kind that really respect the area and take care of the land."

"I can't imagine growing up here."

He smiled. "It was a great place to grow up. I had tons of freedom…after I got all my chores done," he added. "You're going to be a chunk of ice if I don't get you out of this weather."

There was no need for a key as he opened the front door and walked in. The entry was a small, enclosed porch where boots, coats, and hats could be shed and stored, or collected and put on as the weather dictated.

Once he'd toed off his boots and hung his coat and hat on a peg, she followed him into a warm, cozy house with the aroma of a winter fire scenting the air. She had a gas-log fireplace at home that produced more ambiance than heat. She'd spent many hours watching the flames. Still, gas logs didn't come close to replicating the real thing.

A massive fireplace dominated the living room with an enormous television hung over the mantle. Overstuffed leather chairs and sofas filled the space for seating. A wooden coffee table she estimated to be four feet by three feet occupied the open space in front of the sofas. The floor, also wooden, gleamed in the light thrown off by lamps and a small, barely burning fire.

"This way," he said and turned toward a staircase that led to the second level.

She followed him up six steps, turned on a landing and then up an additional staircase. She stepped onto a small landing and then into a long hall.

"My folks' room is to the left," Zane said, gesturing with his chin over his shoulder. He turned to the right. "Eli and I have this end of the house."

She followed him down the hall and stopped when he did in front of three doors.

He gestured with one of her suitcases toward the left. "I'm here. The linen closet is directly in front of you and you're here," he said, opening the door to the right. "This room overlooks the front of the house. Pretty much what you saw coming in."

He entered, set down the two suitcases he carried and turned toward her. "I'll grab the other two. Make yourself at home."

"The bathroom?"

He nodded. "Over here." He walked to a sink in the room. "We each have our own sink. Through here, we share a toilet and shower." He slid the door into the wall exposing a white toilet and shower slash tub combo. "Lori comes in once a week and cleans, but if you need anything before she comes again in a couple of days, don't hesitate to ask."

Wendy pushed her head through the open door and studied the shared bathroom. She figured most women would freak out at these arrangements, but frankly, she'd dressed and undressed for surgery so often with so many different doctors and nurses, she didn't have a shy bone left in her body.

"My parents' room is at the end of the hall. It has its own bathroom if you'd rather the privacy."

She shrugged. "I'm fine. Like I said, I'll sleep tonight and figure out another plan in the morning."

He nodded and left. In a minute, he was setting her other two pieces of luggage in the room.

"I've got a few things I still need to do before calling it a day. Make yourself at home. Dinner's late tonight, so it'll be closer to six-thirty before we eat."

She whirled from where she'd been looking out the window. "Oh. Do I need to fix something?"

He shook his head with a smile. "No. It's baked spaghetti tonight. Everything's been assembled and is ready to bake. I'll pop it in the oven when I get back. I'll see you later." He took a couple of steps and stopped. "Like I said, make yourself at home." He turned to leave but turned back. "I forgot to mention. There are locks on the bathroom doors. I didn't want you to worry." He grinned. "See you at dinner."

She stood at the window and watched him walk toward the big barn on the left. As soon as she knew she was alone, she stripped off the light-weight-perfect-for-Dallas clothes. They were damp and cold and she couldn't wait to get warm again.

There was enough floor space in the room to line her suitcases along a couple of walls and prop them open. It made shifting through her clothing easier. If only she'd thought about grouping the packing either by outfits or all pants together, all shirts together and so forth. Packing so haphazardly wasn't like her. She was a planner, but not this time.

After some digging, she pulled out jeans, thick socks, a white tank top and a green and yellow checked flannel shirt. She briefly considered taking a shower to warm up, but that seemed like a waste of water and electricity. Once dressed, she stepped into the hall and faced her first challenge.

Would it be wrong to look through Zane's door and into his room? His parents' room? She didn't really have much curiosity about his parents' room, but Zane's? Would his bed be made? Since he'd lived here his whole life, would it still look like a high school boy's room with trophies or whatever teen boys decorated their rooms with?

She glanced back into his brother's room. What appeared to be fairly new furniture filled the space. Thick, but obviously worn rugs, covered a glossy wooden floor. The pictures on the walls were photographs she suspected were of this ranch, some taken at ground level, some wide aerial shots. Nothing personal on the tables or wall. Overall, it was a nice guest room that didn't appear to have regular use.

Her gaze flicked back to Zane's door. Her fingers itched to open the door and find answers to her questions. Sneak a quick peek. What could it hurt?

She stiffened her resolve and walked down the stairs, leaving Zane's mysteries behind, whatever they might be. She was here for a night and then she'd leave.

In the living room, a small flicker of a fire waved from the fireplace. She didn't exactly believe in reincarnation, but if there were such a thing, she'd probably been an arsonist in another life. She loved a fire.

It didn't take much effort to haul in a couple of seasoned logs from the back porch. She poked and prodded the embers until the new wood caught flame.

Then, she pulled an overstuffed, soft leather chair closer to the hearth and propped up her feet, letting the heat warm her chilled toes. After a couple of minutes, she found a current magazine for horse ranchers and scanned the table of contents before setting the magazine back on the table.

She settled into the chair's softness and sighed. This mesmerizing fire was the perfect place to relax and think. No patients would call. No surgery prep. No hospital rounds. No weekend call. And she should feel guilty about not missing her medical life, right? Only she didn't. What did that mean?

The warm room, the comfortable chair, and the months of stress combined and overwhelmed her. Her back and shoulder muscles relaxed as her eyes slid shut. Only the occasional neigh from a horse broke the silence.

Now, where did she want to be in five years?

Chapter Four

Z ane stomped his boots on the porch to knock off as much barn muck as he could before removing them and parking them inside the enclosed porch. He'd made the mistake of leaving a pair outside once. Pike and Coda, the ranch border collies, had had a great time with what they'd thought were their new chew toys. He couldn't blame them, however. He'd been the fool to leave them within the reach of their teeth.

Speaking of his dogs, Zane's gaze swept across the pastures for the working pair, but saw no sign of them. As he began pursing his lips to whistle for them, two loud, shrill whistles blasted from the barn. Then he heard the barks as the dogs moved side to side and around the horses in the field. Working as a team, they moved the horses down the fenced area and through the gate Cowboy Russ had standing open. The ten horses trotted through the gate and into the barn, the two black and white dogs close on their heels. Once their roundup work was completed, Pike and Coda raced from the barn toward the main house.

He laughed as they hit the porch at full speed and then skidded to a stop at the toes of his socks.

"Okay. Let me see those feet if you want to come in the house."

Both dogs dropped on their bellies, rolled on their sides, and put their paws in the air, a neat trick his mother had taught them. Muddy paws made muddy tracks through the house, so she'd trained Pike and Coda to let her clean their feet.

He retrieved the dog towel from the enclosed porch and cleaned eight paws. As soon as he was done, the dogs jumped back to their feet ready to head inside for dinner. Freely available meals, like dog food, had the potential to attract some unwanted wildlife visitors—a valuable lesson learned over the years. Now, the dogs were fed either inside the house or inside their kennels, which were accessed via a small room under the stairwell. Heated in the winter with excellent air flow in the summer, their kennels were more akin to dog palaces, not that the two spent much time in them. They were too busy running the ranch, or so they would tell you if they could talk.

"Okay, let's see what we can fix you two for dinner," he said, walking into the house. "No steak, Pike," he said, and the dog's eyes took on a look of pity that made Zane chuckle. He had no idea the size of their vocabulary, but he knew they understood more than some of the people he worked with in Chicago.

For the first time since frigid temperatures took hold, a warm room greeted his entrance. From the kitchen, he noticed the fireplace had fresh wood and a nice blaze going. Parked in front of the hearth was his mother's favorite chair—what she called her reading chair. Long, blonde hair draped over the arm. He shushed the dogs and quietly made his way over to the chair.

Wendy's shapely legs were stretched out with socked feet propped on the rock hearth. Her slender fingers were interlaced and lay across her stomach. Then his gaze stopped on her face. Whew. He'd just about convinced himself she wasn't as gorgeous as he'd originally thought. He was oh so wrong about that. The woman was still a knockout beauty, but asleep, some of the stress on her face had been erased. His heart rattled like the tail end of a rattlesnake.

Yeah, he wasn't going there. She might be beautiful. Her personality might shine like a full moon, not that he'd spent enough time with her to know. She might have a body that filled a man's fantasy. Hell, she might be as rich as Croesus, but none of that mattered. He was not getting involved with someone like her…rich, beautiful, and pampered, not to mention a recently jilted bride. No thank you. Been there. Had the scars to prove it. He was smarter now than he'd been in Chicago, or at best, more cautious.

As he was considering how to wake her without scaring her to death, Coda decided she was the perfect alarm clock. She sniffed Wendy's hair, then put her paws on the arm of the chair and licked up the side of Wendy's face.

Since he wasn't sure what Wendy's reaction would be, he headed back to the kitchen to play innocent. Let Coda take the blame.

"Hey," a sleepy voice said. "Where'd you come from?"

"You awake?" he called.

"Hard to sleep with a dog licking my face. I'm not complaining, mind you. Just stating a fact. She's beautiful. Who is she? Wait, there's another one. Who are these cuties?"

Zane pulled a beer from the fridge. "The bigger one is Pike. The other is Coda. Want a beer?" He almost groaned. *Of course she won't want a beer.* "Or there's probably some wine around here."

"Beer's fine," she said, standing and stretching her arms over her head, then adding a yawn at the end.

He was glad to see she'd changed into clothing more suitable to the Montana winter.

He pulled out another beer and passed it to her as she walked into the kitchen, Pike and Coda on her heels. "Looks like you've got a couple of fans," he said, gesturing to the dogs with his bottle.

She smiled and leaned down to hug each dog. "They know a sucker when they see one, I guess." She stood. "I hope you don't mind that I added wood to the fire and sort of rearranged the chair. I love to watch a fire burn. It's something with the flames, I think. So calming and mesmerizing." She chuckled. "Someone could probably hypnotize me with a fire."

"I don't mind at all. I told you to make yourself at home. Plus, it was nice coming home to a warm house that didn't involve spending a small fortune on electricity."

"Now, dinner. What can I do to help? You said something about a spaghetti casserole."

"Oven's on." He pointed to the dial he'd flipped before grabbing his beer. "Thirty minutes, and it's done."

"What can I do to help?"

He shrugged. "Lori is always trying to force me to eat salads. I usually end up tossing the lettuce and tomatoes. If you want, I'm sure there's salad makings in the fridge. Help yourself to that."

"A good salad never killed anyone. Who knows? It could be healthy, and you might like it."

She pulled out fresh romaine lettuce, cherry tomatoes, a carrot and a sad-looking cucumber. "Not sure about this cucumber, but the rest will work."

He slid the heavy pan into the oven and closed the door. "I hate cucumbers. I don't know why she buys them."

"Good," she said with a smile. "I hate them, too. Where's the trash can? That's where this thing belongs."

While the casserole cooked, he took the dogs to their kennels, prepared their dinner, and left them there to eat. He knew from personal experience that they wouldn't beg at the table, but some guests still felt the need to slip the dogs treats off their plates, which was a firm no in this house.

He dug into his mom's deep freezer and found a loaf of garlic bread frozen so hard he was fairly confident he could use it as a bat and hit a homerun. But he'd seen his mom do magic with something like this. Surely he could, too?

"Whatcha got there?" Wendy asked as she chopped lettuce for the salad.

He held up his prize. "Garlic bread. Date unknown. Length of time in freezer unknown. Shall we risk it?"

"Sure. What do the baking directions say?"

"There are directions?" he joked.

She laughed. "Spoken like a guy." Holding out her hand, she wiggled her fingers. "Gimme and let me see."

Her blue eyes sparkled as she read the directions on the metallic bag. He was sure there hadn't been a sparkle there when he'd picked her up earlier today.

"Okay," she said. "Four-fifty. Ten minutes. How long on the spaghetti?"

"Ten minutes."

"Go ahead and bump up the temp and let's add this. The coldness will slow down the spaghetti's cooking while this thaws and browns."

Dinner might have been—no, correction—it was the best meal he'd had since his parents left. He was used to dining alone, sometimes in front of the television, or sometimes with a book on his tablet, but that didn't mean he enjoyed it. He'd missed the give-and-take of social conversation. A meal that would have taken him fifteen minutes to scarf down in front of the television took over an hour tonight. He steered clear of weddings and the whole jilted-bride thing. He couldn't imagine how she must have felt. He noticed she didn't bring it up either, so it seemed to him that they were on the same page.

After dinner, he insisted she go enjoy the fire. He would toss everything into the dishwasher and be done with it.

"Can I let the dogs back in?" she asked.

"Sure. They sleep in the house anyway."

Pointing to the small door under the stairs, she asked, "Through here, right?"

He nodded. He was touched she'd thought about Pike and Coda and hadn't just rushed back to her chair and given them no thought.

She was laughing when she came back into the room. Pike and Coda were thrilled to have a new human to lavish love and praises on them. Her laugh sent warning signals to his gut because damned if he didn't like the sound. She had a pull toy in her hand, and Pike was determined, sort of, to get it away from her. Racing to the living room with the toy over her head, her socks slid on the glossy wood floor, and she crashed into the back of the chair she'd been using.

He dropped the dishtowel and headed that way until he heard her chuckling and talking to the dogs.

"God, I almost lost it. Did you guys see that?" She shook the toy at them. "Still want this, do you? Well, come on."

With that, Pike jumped onto the chair and was high enough to snatch the toy from her hands and race away. Coda barked and ran after him.

She fell into the chair with an "Oomph."

"You okay?" he called to her.

"Yeah. Those two are something."

"Border collies usually are. Almost too smart sometimes. Remind me to show you how they work in the fields. It's pretty amazing."

"Sounds interesting."

He walked into the living room. "I have to get up at six in the morning, so if you don't mind, I think I'll call it a night. I'll shower and then the bathroom is all yours."

She waved a hand over the back of the chair. "I totally understand. You don't mind if I stay here for a while?"

"Nope. I'll go ahead and lock up. Want me to throw a log on the fire before I do?"

"I don't think so. I'll go to bed shortly."

"Good night then."

"Night."

He whistled for the dogs, and the three of them headed up the stairs. As much as he would have enjoyed spending more time with Wendy, mornings came early, and the forecast for tomorrow's weather was nasty.

Chapter Five

W endy spent the next thirty minutes after Zane
went to bed poking the fire and thinking
about the past year. Her life was off-track. She wasn't
sure if this hiccup was personal or professional, but
wasn't that why she'd come up here in the middle of
nowhere in the dead of winter? To think? To plan?
To hide?

No, definitely not to hide.

Well, maybe hiding was part of it. Lately, she'd
found herself majorly dissatisfied with her life.

Was she still happy being a doctor? She couldn't
honestly say. She'd had her fill of rhinoplasties,
facelifts, and eye jobs. She lived for the patients who
really needed her talents, like breast reconstruction
patients, or trauma patients who needed skin and
tissue pieced back together to minimize scarring, but
those were not her bread-and-butter patients. If she

could do it all over again, would she still want to be a doctor?

The memory of why she went into medicine made her wince. At age nine, her sister had announced she was going to be a doctor. Wendy had immediately shouted, "Me too," because she and Risa always did everything together. From that day forward, she never considered any other career path. They went to the same college, joined the same sorority, roomed together, and took many of the same classes together. Medical school followed a strikingly similar pattern. Until today, she'd never given much thought to a life that didn't have her sister as her closest friend and neighbor.

The hard question she needed to answer was *had she become a doctor only because Risa had?* She honestly wasn't sure, but she thought maybe so. When she decided as a child that medicine was her life goal and she refused to explore other jobs and careers, had she closed potential doors of opportunity? She understood herself enough to be fully aware that her plastic-surgery specialty was directly related to Risa's interest in researching and treating breast cancer.

If Risa had chosen a different field, would Wendy have followed suit? Maybe. No, the real answer was probably, and that realization made her stomach sour.

What if there'd been no Risa, no twin to share her life, no decision to become a doctor at age nine? What would she have studied in college? Computers? Accounting? Fashion merchandising?

Or would she have followed her love of animals

and become a veterinarian? As much as she loved all the conveniences of her Dallas condo, she missed living on her family's ranch and all the animals there. Missed the freedom to climb on a horse and ride. Missed listening to the crack of the leather, the clop of each step, the whistle of air rushing past her ear when she let the horse fly.

She'd never known, and hoped she would never know, life without Risa. However, she wished she could experience some of the contentedness she knew her sister felt with her life. Was she blocked from that degree of happiness because she wasn't following her own path in life? Was it possible that she wasn't living the life she was supposed to live? Was some of her discontentment because she'd followed Risa's life plan and was now living Risa's choices instead of her own?

She couldn't say. She only knew she hated her feelings of jealousy about her sister's wonderful life, which was completely unfair to Risa. Her life hadn't been always perfect. She'd gone through her fair share of disappointments before Trevor and their new son. The last time she'd seen her sister before leaving, her eyes shone with a sparkle Wendy couldn't remember ever seeing before. Risa's life was charging down the road of happiness and success.

Sometimes Wendy felt like her downs in life were deeper and longer than any Risa had ever had.

As that last thought crossed her mind, she chuckled and shook her head. This might be the best-attended pity party she'd ever thrown for herself.

Fine then. She would get her head together before

she went home. She would not be a dark rain cloud on everyone around her.

A jaw-popping yawn stopped her musings. She needed to sleep. Her short nap today didn't begin to make up for all the late nights and early mornings she'd put in since telling her partners she was taking some leave. Surely Zane had had enough time to shower and vacate the bathroom.

A tiny smile twitched at the corner of her mouth. If he hadn't, and she hurried up there, she might catch him au naturel. Not that she hadn't seen more than her fair share of naked men. She had, but holy moly! She bet he had a six-pack that no gym workout could produce.

She sighed. Enough. Time for bed.

After securing the fireplace screen, she moved the chair back to its proper location and climbed the stairs. As cold as it was, she should have requested a dog bed partner.

All was quiet upstairs and the light was off in the bathroom when she entered her bedroom. She brushed her teeth and decided to shower in the morning. Then she collapsed into the soft sheets and dropped off quickly to sleep.

When she woke, the darkness in the room confused her, as did the bed and the furniture. It took a couple of minutes to put all the pieces together. She slid upright in the bed and pulled her phone over to check the time. Three a.m. Four a.m. at home.

She thought about getting up. It wouldn't be the first time she'd been up and out of bed at this hour.

But why? She had no schedule to keep. No medical journals that she needed to read. No surgery to prep for. She could get up and research hotels and inns in the area, she reminded herself, but instead, she nestled back into the warm sheets and let herself drop off again.

The next time she woke, bright fingers of sunlight poked through the drapes and jabbed at her eyes. Her stomach growled loudly, like a dragon demanding to be fed. She stretched out her arms and legs as far as possible and groaned as her back gave her a satisfying pop. It was only then she looked at the time on her phone and her mouth gaped in surprise. It was eleven forty-five. Closer to lunch time than breakfast. Her host must have wondered where she was by now.

After a quick shower, she dressed and headed downstairs, her wet hair hanging limply down her back. She expected to find she had the house to herself, so she startled when she found Zane leaning on a kitchen counter eating a sandwich.

"Good afternoon, princess."

"Sorry. Didn't mean to sleep so late."

He shrugged. "No problem." Using the last quarter of his sandwich, he gestured toward the single-serve coffee pot. "Coffee's there. Cream in the fridge. Sugar in the cabinet above the pot."

She nodded. "Thanks. Black's fine."

He continued to eat while her coffee dripped. As soon as she could, she jerked the cup from under the spout and took a large gulp, burning her tongue in the process.

"Want a sandwich? Or there's breakfast stuff in the cabinets and fridge."

"I'm not really hungry." Her stomach took that moment to roar like a lion.

He gave her a pointed look, as though saying, "Really?"

"Sandwich it is," she said. Since the bread, condiments, meats, and cheeses were already on the counter, it seemed the most logical choice.

"The day's half gone," he observed.

She nodded as she bit into her turkey, ham, and cheese sandwich and chewed.

"A little late to be trying to find a motel in the area today, especially with the snow forecast." He studied her. "You ever been on a horse?"

She startled at the abrupt change of subject. "I've ridden."

She didn't want to brag, but she'd grown up on a ranch, and had been on the back of horses since she'd been inside her mom's uterus.

He nodded. "Great. I could use a little help today. One of my regular guys is out with a sick kid."

"Oh, no. That's awful."

Before she could ask any medical questions about the child's symptoms, he continued. "I need to get a couple of horses out for some exercise. These two are pampered pets whose owner didn't get them ready for a Montana winter, so I need to give them a little exercise before putting them back in their stalls. Want to take a thirty-minute ride or so? It'd be a great help."

She thought about it for a full thirty seconds,

maybe less, before smiling. "I'd love to. Give me ten minutes." She swept her hand down her body. "Need to dry my hair and dress for riding."

She was already to the landing when he asked, "You have boots, right? Or do I need to find some for you?"

"Got 'em. Be right back."

She could do hotel research tonight and move tomorrow. What's one more day?

By the time she got back downstairs, Zane had already headed out. After wrapping a cashmere scarf around her neck, she slipped on her heavy coat, and pulled a knit hat down on her head. Icy-cold air slapped her cheeks as soon as she stepped onto the porch. Memories of Colorado ski vacations brought a smile to her lips. How long had it been since she'd skied? Three years? No, wait, over six years. Wow. Where had the time gone? Every year she promised herself she'd get away from the office, but now that she thought about it, wow. It'd been at least six years since she'd taken a vacation. No wonder her staff had been shocked when she took this leave of absence.

The driveway between the house and the barn was sloppy and muddy. It'd snowed last night, and today's traffic had produced a path of dirty muck. Still, the mountain peaks in the distance were a bright white against the deep-blue sky. The view was breathtaking and she allowed herself a couple of minutes just to soak it in.

The clop of horses brought her attention back to

the porch and she glanced to her left. Zane was riding a gray while leading a buckskin-colored horse.

"This one's Maddie," he said, lifting the reins on the gray. "She's a prima donna bitch." He lifted the reins of the buckskin. "This one is Albert. He's a sweetheart gelding. A real flirt. I think you'll like him."

"I'm sure I will." She bounded down the steps into the yard, thankful for the sparse grass in the snow even if it was crispy dead. "Hi, Albert," she cooed, rubbing the gelding's nose. "Ready to see some pretty countryside?"

Albert snorted as though agreeing.

Wendy laughed. "We're going to get along fine."

"Need help getting on?"

Wendy swung into the saddle with ease. "Nope. I've got it." She took the reins from him and smiled. "I'm ready." A horse between her legs felt as natural as a scalpel in her hand.

He studied her like he was trying to see into her mind, and then he nodded. Turning Maddie around, he headed for the drive.

She and Albert followed. From this angle, she had an impressive view, and she didn't mean of the countryside. Her host had broad shoulders that pulled his all-weather coat snug. A worn ballcap sat atop his silver-streaked, dark hair. His comfort in the saddle bespoke years of experience, which wasn't surprising given he'd been born, raised, and never left here.

She had questions about her host. Lots of questions. Had he gone to college? Been married? Had a serious relationship? Was he in a serious relationship now? Not that any of that mattered in the least. She was only going to stay another day or so, and he certainly hadn't been giving off any sign that he was interested in asking those questions of her. So what if the hard angles of his face and that slight bump on his nose were her cup of tea? Didn't matter. She needed to be thinking about her future, not her present.

It might have been over half-a-decade since she'd skied, but it'd been only a couple of months since she'd ridden. The clop of the horse hooves in the mucky gravel was a soothing tonic to her soul. Maybe she should have made time to go home to the ranch more often. Her shoulders relaxed; the headache she'd been fighting for the last month eased. She drew in a deep breath and exhaled.

"You okay back there?" Zane asked over his shoulder.

"Perfect."

"There's plenty of room to ride alongside me." He reined Maddie to a halt and waited for Wendy to ride up beside him. Once she was, he clicked his tongue and they rode out onto the gravel road.

"This place is beautiful. Tell me more about the ranch."

He glanced toward her. "Sure. What do you want to know?"

"How long has your family been here?"

"My great-granddad, Charlie Miller, bought the land in the late eighteen hundreds, more as an investment than for ranching. He and my great-grandmother lived right outside the north entrance to

Yellowstone Park. He ran a small mercantile. Unfortunately, Great-Grandpa Charlie was shot by a customer over an outstanding bill and died. My great-grandmother, Shirley, didn't have much in the way of marketable skills and couldn't handle the store and seven children. So my granddad, Thomas Miller, dropped out of school, and the family moved into an old shack on this property. Grandpa Thomas started boarding horses and the Grizzly Bitterroot was born."

Her eyes opened wide. "That's an incredible story. What happened to the other children and your great-grandmother?"

They reined the horses to the left and began walking up a slight incline.

"Granddad had a couple of sisters who died. I don't know if it's the truth, but granddad said they died from strep throat."

She nodded. "I believe it. Back then, we didn't have the antibiotics we do now."

"My great-grandparents are buried about a mile up the road, along with four of the children. The two girls who died from illness, a son who fell off a horse and, again according to my granddad, broke his fool neck, and another daughter who died from the flu. The last brother left Montana and went to Wyoming. His branch of the family settled around Pikeson."

"That's quite a history." She gestured toward the surrounding hills and pastures. "Growing up here must have been wonderful."

He chuckled. "Oh, you have no idea the trouble ranch boys can get into."

She laughed. "I have a few ideas, but I'd love to hear some stories."

When they rode back down the drive, forty-five minutes had passed. The sun had hidden behind some dark clouds, and the wind began to whip around. She would swear the temperature had fallen at least twenty degrees, but that was probably her imagination.

"See the clouds? Feel the change?" he asked.

"What?" She looked up. "Those clouds? Yeah. I did notice them. Is it my imagination or is it colder?"

"Colder. Gonna get more snow."

"Oh." Her voice arched with surprise. "So early in winter? Wait, it's not even winter yet. That doesn't come for another ten days or so. It's still officially fall."

He laughed. "Tell that to Mother Nature. She loves to begin her winters in Montana in November, and when she's really bitchy, October, so I feel lucky to have had such great weather so far."

She studied the gloomy skies. "Great weather?"

He nodded with a chuckle. "It's been nice for this time of the year. Go ahead and ride to the house. I'll take Albert back to the barn."

"No, no. That's okay. Albert and I have a deal. He gives me a good ride, and I make sure he's brushed and gets a treat."

One eyebrow arched. "You know how to unsaddle and brush a horse?"

This time, it was she who chuckled. "Mr. Miller. You have no idea what all I know."

Chapter Six

❧❦❧

Zane arched an eyebrow and grinned. "You don't say. Well, I look forward to discovering all you know, Wendy McCool."

She laughed, and they rode to the barn. She slipped off the horse like a pro and gathered Albert's reins.

During his ride with Wendy, Zane realized she was more experienced with horses than he'd anticipated. Since she lived in Dallas—a huge city with heavy traffic, tall buildings, millions of people, and no horses—he hadn't expected her to handle Albert like she had.

However, she'd swung into the saddle like someone who'd done it a million times, with ease and without thought. Her boots, while bearing the looks of recent polish, still showed signs of use with their worn and scuffed leather. Everything about how she carried herself on Albert's back screamed *experienced rider*. She had a better seat than some of his cowboys.

They rode into the barn, and she slipped off Albert's back. "Which way?"

He understood her confusion. Their barn had started as a single aisle with stalls on either side. Over the years, the place had been improved and added on to a number of times. Now there were hallways going in different directions and stalls for thirty horses, not that they kept the horses indoors all winter. But some owners insisted on fancy stalls with access to private exercise yards, and they were willing to pay premium prices to get it. If there was one thing he understood, it was money.

"This way. Albert has a place in the new wing."

Her eyebrows rose. "Sounds fancy."

Zane laughed. "If Albert's owner thought Albert would enjoy a sofa in his digs, I swear she would buy him one."

Wendy rubbed the gelding's nose. "Lucky boy."

"He is," Zane agreed.

"What about Maddie?"

"Her owner adores her, too, but she's a tad more realistic about horses." He stopped and Wendy halted.

"This is Maddie's palace," he said, gesturing to a standard stall.

"Poor Maddie," Wendy joked. "Standard stall."

He led the horse into the space and closed the lower portion of the half-door. "Be right back," he cooed to the mare. She eyed him like she was trying to decide whether he was telling the truth. "I promise," he said.

He pointed down the hall. "This way. I'll walk you to Prince Albert's castle."

She laughed. "I think I might like Albert's person."

He nodded. "You probably would. She lives in California and comes to Montana to get away from the crowds. She has a few horses, but Albert was her first, and so far, no one, nor any horse, can take his place."

"I understand completely."

They exited through the rear of the main barn. "We could have actually gone around, but I thought you might enjoy the tour." He pointed to the right. "That's the west wing and—" he pointed to the left, "—the east wing. We are in the process of building some new stables closer to the summer rentals."

"Summer rentals?"

"Cabins. We have a small but growing dude-ranch business, something my brother and I are building for when he gets out of the SEALs."

"Maybe I could stay up there instead of invading your house."

He shook his head. "Sorry. They really are summer only at this time. You would not only freeze to death, but we have all the utilities shut off for winter. Once Eli gets home, the plan is to work toward year-round dude ranching."

He led them into the west wing and walked her and Albert along a brick floor toward an area of ten private stalls, each with its own access to a private grazing area. On the way, they passed the wash bay, the newish medical bay, and Zane's office.

"I'm not usually impressed with barns and stables." She looked at him. "You might have figured out that I've seen a few."

He smiled. "Yes, I realized quickly this is not your first rodeo."

She chuckled. "Grew up on a ranch outside of Dallas. Nearest town was a place called Diamond Lakes. I might have been a better water skier if I hadn't spent so much time on horseback."

"How many acres?"

"Not huge. My parents inherited it from my mom's parents. I think there is about two hundred acres, maybe?" She shrugged. "I swear I don't remember. They lease out a large section of the property for cattle grazing. They kept about forty acres or so near the house for a barn, some corrals and riding trails."

"Sounds nice."

"It is." She gestured around. "I guess it was like growing up here, only fewer acres."

"My parents have done a ton of work on the place, trust me." He stopped at a white half-door. "Here we are."

Wendy opened the lower door and looked around. "Nice. Looks like fresh straw and water has already been done."

He nodded. "Yeah. Had a couple of guys out early this morning. Once you get him unsaddled, would you mind brushing and rubbing him down?"

"Of course not. Honestly, Zane. This makes me happy. I love working with the horses. The scent of straw and manure brings back a ton of great memories from home."

"I appreciate your help."

"Hey, it's the least I can do."

He nodded. "I'll leave you to it. I've got Maddie waiting on me and I promise, she will be pissed."

She was laughing as he walked away.

He brushed Maddie and made sure she had food and water. Cowboy Russ stopped him as Zane walked past the old barn office where they now stored grains and oats.

The men spent the next half-hour going over the boarding calendar and work schedules for the next couple of weeks. Once they were done, Zane headed back to Albert's stall to check on Wendy. Albert was munching away, his coat shiny from Wendy's care.

"You're a lucky guy, Albert," he told the horse.

Albert eyed him, snorted, and went back to his dinner.

Speaking of dinner, Zane's stomach growled. He was famished. As he exited the boarding area, he checked in each stall and found only contented horses who didn't wish to be disturbed.

At the house, he toed off his boots and set them inside the mudroom porch. After shucking his coat, hat, and gloves, he headed into the house.

"Now, I'm not sure that Zane would agree with you," he heard Wendy say. He wondered who she was talking to and what he wouldn't agree with.

"Don't give me those sad eyes, Pike. I know good

and well you were fed. And you know good and well that this chicken casserole isn't for you."

The border collie whined and then barked his disagreement.

"Look at how good Coda's being."

Pike barked again and Zane laughed.

"That dog's a liar," he said to Wendy as he walked into the kitchen.

The two dogs sprang to their feet and rushed over to Zane, jumping on him and barking.

"That's enough," he said, stopping to pet each dog. Then he pulled a couple of dog treats from a jar and handed one to each of them. Once they had their treats, they plopped down on the floor to eat.

"They are very sweet," Wendy said.

"Spoiled rotten."

She smiled. "I know they're working dogs, but I like that they get to be house dogs at night."

"Don't blame me. That's all my mom's doing. She's a soft touch."

With a slight shrug, she said, "I think she must be very kind. After all, didn't she offer up her ranch to me just because I needed to get away?"

He laughed. "Kind? She didn't whip your legs with a switch when you were growing up."

"Why do I think you probably deserved it?"

He forced his face into a shocked expression. "I assure you. I was nothing short of a dream child."

She chuckled. "Uh-huh. What's the age difference between you and your brother?"

"Two years."

"How bad were the tussles when you were young?"

He shook his head. "Epic."

"So, you're saying, your mom had her hands full with the two of you? And maybe the switch was to get your attention?"

"Better than getting my dad involved," he said.

His stomach took that moment to let out a loud protest. He pressed his hand to his gut. "Sorry about that."

"Hungry?"

"Starved. Hey, I've got an idea. Let's go into town and have dinner. There's a decent steak place in Gardiner."

He didn't know where that invitation came from. It wasn't as though he'd been thinking about asking her out. His eyes saw an attractive woman and his mouth moved before his brain was fully engaged. Still, it wasn't a bad idea. Today, they'd talked about him growing up and the ranch. He'd avoided the topic of her being left at the altar by not asking her anything about herself, but that wasn't working for him. He was curious about her, and over dinner, he could steer the conversation her way.

"Thanks, Zane. That's a nice offer, but Lori left us a chicken enchilada casserole. It's ready to go into the oven and there's some fresh bread she baked to go with it." Wendy waved a piece of paper from the bar. "Here's the cooking instructions. I didn't start it because I didn't know when you'd be in and if you'd want to eat so early."

"Okay," he said, disappointed but not deterred.

"And for the record, yes, we usually eat early around here. Mornings come early, which means hitting the sack early, so dinner between four and five is normal."

"Okay then. I wasn't sure. I'll turn the oven on for the casserole. I assume you've done this before?"

"Cooked one of Lori's casseroles? Oh, yeah. Probably four times a week. Without Russ's wife, I'd probably eat cold cereal every night."

"Super. If you'll excuse me, I'm going to head up and get a shower…unless you want to go first."

With a wave of his hand toward the stairs, he said, "Go on. Holler if you need something."

As soon as her trim ass turned the corner and disappeared from view, he sagged against the counter. It'd been a while since a woman had turned him down for dinner. Hell…he reflected over the past ten years. Not one. Maybe he was losing his touch now that he was back on the ranch.

He slipped the loaded dish into the oven and set the timer. As he pulled a bottle of beer from the fridge, his cell phone trilled. One glance at the caller readout, and he groaned before answering.

"Hello, Priscilla." He twisted off the cap and flipped it into the garbage.

"Zane, darling, it's so good to hear your voice. I miss you so much."

More like she missed his wallet so much. He'd met Priscilla at a friend's Christmas gala three years ago. They'd clicked like pieces of a puzzle, or so he'd thought. It was only after they'd gotten engaged that he realized he didn't know the real woman under all that long, shiny black hair and fabulous body. Oh, he was sure she loved him, but he was even more sure that she loved what he could do for her. Chicago society was her favorite playground, and that world took loads of money and influence. In Zane, she'd found both.

For a while, he'd enjoyed the lavish parties, the noteworthy fundraisers, and even seeing Priscilla and himself in society photographs. However, the stressful days at the office combined with the never-ending merry-go-round of nightly appearances had worn him down. When he'd suggested they skip some event, Priscilla would have a complete meltdown at the idea, and so he would go.

The social networking had been crucial to his success as an investment banker and finally a hedge fund manager. He had Priscilla to thank for that. However, after a couple of years of nonstop going, he'd just begun to do some serious life reflection when his mother fell ill. His parents had encouraged him to continue living his life and not to worry about them, but after eighteen months, he'd seen the strain his mom's illness was taking on both his parents. He'd come home to help, and other than the one trip back to his Chicago condo to pack his essentials, he'd not been back.

That'd been six months ago, and Priscilla still held hope he would "come to his senses,", as she liked to put it, and come home to Chicago.

He wasn't going back. He'd been quite firm on that point with her.

"I told you that you were welcome to come to Montana for a visit," he said, walking into the office and closing the door.

He knew that was a hollow offer. There was no way she would leave Chicago, except maybe for New York, or Miami or LA.

"Why would I come there?" she said in a whiny voice he hadn't missed at all. "You know I can't stand the smell of horses or barns. When are you coming home? I miss you."

He tipped the bottle back and let the cold brew flow down his throat. "Again, Pris, I'm not coming back to Chicago. In fact, I've been giving serious thought to selling my condo."

She gasped. "But what about me? What about us?"

He sighed and sat in the rolling desk chair.

Priscilla had her own home, but she didn't feel her condo fit her view of where a woman of society should live. Only Zane's multi-million-dollar condo would do.

"Well, there is no us, as you told me when you threw the engagement ring in my face. And you have your own condo, so there's that."

She huffed and he knew she'd been using his place —without his permission—as her residence. Fancier and more impressive, she'd once told him.

But he and Eli needed the money he'd get from the sale of his condo to continue with the development of Grizzly Bitterroot Dude Ranch.

"I thought you loved me," she cried into the phone and then sniffed.

Yeah, he'd fallen for that fake cry and sniffing too many times. No more. Besides, he'd regretted the engagement almost from the moment it'd happened. Looking back, he wasn't exactly sure how they'd come to be engaged. He was fairly certain it hadn't been his idea.

"You'll always be special to me, but you need to move on. My home is in Montana and yours is in Chicago. I know the right guy is out there for you. It's just not me."

"You're really not coming back, are you?"

"No." He made sure his voice was firm and without hesitation.

She sighed. "I'd better go. There's a party at the Willhams' tonight and I need to get dressed."

"Priscilla, take care of yourself. I'm here if you need a friend or to talk."

"I really am going to miss you, Zane."

"Take care."

He ended the call and set the phone on the desk. As he reached to turn on the computer, the buzzer from the oven went off. Great. He was starving.

Plus, if he was lucky, he'd have company for dinner.

Chapter Seven

W endy combed out her wet hair and debated dinner. The way she saw it, she had two choices. She could go downstairs and eat a luscious casserole someone else had made or sit in her room and listen to her belly grumble. Not really much to decide, was there?

She quickly dried her hair before dressing in leggings, a long sweater, socks, and slipped on her UGGs. The oven timer buzzed as she walked down the stairs.

"Smells yummy," she said, entering the kitchen.

Zane set the hot dish on the stove and removed a pair of oven mitts. "And very, very hot," he said.

"Want me to set the table?"

"Sure." He pointed to a set of cabinets. "Plates and glasses there. Silverware in this drawer."

The utensils clattered as she jerked open a drawer.

"There's wine in the fridge, if you want it," he

continued. "Beer, too. Probably some milk, if we're lucky. I'm going to run up and take a quick shower before I eat."

"I'll wait for you." She ate enough dinners alone. Having someone else to talk to was a treat.

"I'd like that. I promise to be speedy."

"I'll wait."

A bright smile lifted the corners of his lips and put a twinkle in his eyes. "Great."

He hurried out of the room, and she heard his feet fall heavily on the stairs as he rushed up.

After setting the kitchen table, she stood in front of the opened refrigerator door, debating what to drink. Finally, she pulled a chilled white wine from the shelf and rattled around through drawers until she found the wine opener. It was only after she got the cork out that she realized she knew where the glasses and mugs were, but she hadn't seen any wineglasses. Would Zane think her totally classless if she poured her wine into a mug? After all, a mug would hide exactly how much wine she was drinking, right?

"Mom keeps her good wineglasses in the cabinet over the sink."

Wendy whirled around. "Wow. That has to have been a world record shower."

Zane's wet hair had been combed straight back off his face. He wore a pair of jeans that told the story of hundreds of washings and a gray sweatshirt. The only thing on his feet were socks. No shoes. He looked good enough to... Well, eat.

Patting his stomach, he said, "I'm starving."

"I didn't make a salad. After watching you move the lettuce around on your plate last night, I have come to the conclusion that you aren't much of a salad guy."

With a twist at the corner of his mouth, he said, "Poor Lori. She loads my fridge with fresh veggies every week, and every week, they get fed to the animals."

Wendy was tall, but she had to stand on her toes to reach into the cabinet storing the wine glasses. "You want wine?"

"Sure. You need me to get those?"

"Nope. I've got it." She lifted two glasses down and studied them. "Um, how long have these been up there?"

He shrugged. "No clue. Might want to rinse them out."

"My thoughts exactly."

Once they were seated at the table, she poured two generous glasses of wine.

"Cheers," she said, lifting her glass, which he immediately clinked.

"I guess you're wondering why Mom stored those glasses up there."

Using a spatula, Wendy lifted a couple of the chicken enchiladas and plopped them onto his plate and then did the same for her.

"I was wondering about the glasses, but I wasn't going to be nosy."

"When Eli and I were younger, the only way Mom could get us to drink milk was to put it into the fancy glasses." He grinned, and her heart skipped a beat or ten. "That's what we called wineglasses, but it wasn't enough to just drink out of them. We had to give lots of toasts and clink our glasses. After we broke about six of her good ones, she bought some cheap ones and put her good ones up there, thinking Eli and I would never find them." He shook his head.

"How long did it take you to find them?"

"Maybe ten minutes. What about you? Brothers? Sisters?"

"Sister."

"Are you close in age?"

She laughed. "You could say that. She's older by ten minutes."

His eyes widen. "Twins? Really? How'd I miss that tidbit? Identical?"

"Yeah, pretty much, but she's the prettier twin."

"I don't see how that's possible," he said, before shoving a large bite of casserole into his mouth.

His comment made her sit straighter in her chair and she smiled. "Why, thank you, sir, but hard to believe given my current attire and hair."

He pointed his fork at her. "Don't be modest. You have a mirror."

Before she could reply, there was a knock at the door.

"'Cuse me." He blotted his lips with a napkin and stood.

For the first time in her life, she was jealous of a paper napkin.

She continued with her dinner, not sure how long he would be away. As it turned out, he was back quickly, only his face wore an agitated expression. He jabbed at a piece of the casserole, his fork tines clanking on the plate.

"What's wrong?"

He looked up. "Sorry. I'm irritated."

"Want to talk about it?"

He chewed and took a long gulp of wine. He refilled his glass almost to the rim and took another drink.

His lips tightened into a straight line and then he said, "One of my regular cowboys, Josh Madden, got into a fight tonight over a woman." His voice was harsh with frustration. "My bet is on too much beer and lack of brains. Anyway, his right arm is broken as is his left cheekbone. He'll be out of commission for a few days."

"Days? Sounds like it might be weeks."

He shrugged. "Maybe."

"No maybe about it."

He jabbed another piece of enchilada and shoved it between his lips—full lips that looked perfect for long sessions of kissing and—

Stop it. You are here to think and reflect. Not hit on the handsome cowboy.

As before, he pointed his fork at her. "You handled Albert great today."

"Thanks." She felt him working up to something.

"You said you missed the ranch."

Nodding, she said, "True."

He smiled, and his whole appearance changed. "I've got an idea."

"Uh-huh."

"Maybe you could stay here a little longer before moving to a hotel and…and, you know, help out with the horses."

"You want me to muck stalls?"

He flinched. "Well, maybe one or two, or maybe I can get those, and you can help with food, water, and exercise."

She laughed. "Zane. I've mucked more stalls for more years than I have fingers. I mean, it's not my favorite thing to do on a ranch, but it makes me happy to know I can do something for my horses, you know?"

"One of the realities of ranch life."

"True." She blew out a long breath. "Let me sleep on it, okay? I'll give you an answer in the morning."

"Fair enough. I usually start the day between five-thirty and six. Plus, you won't be the only female tomorrow. Sally Carter and Lynne Bailey come on Wednesdays."

When she furrowed her brow, he continued.

"Some of the owners help out here as a way to save money on their boarding fees. Sally and Lynne always come on Wednesdays, Saturdays, and Sundays."

"Are they the only owners to do that?"

"Oh, no. Beth comes on Mondays, Thursdays and the weekends. Elizabeth and Mary help out on Fridays. And…" His eyes rolled up and to the left as he thought. "There are a couple of sisters named Fran and Gail who come on Monday and Tuesday."

She laughed. "All women?"

He chuckled. "Well, there are some guys, too, but I thought you'd want to know about the females so you wouldn't be nervous about being the only woman."

"I'll let you know in the morning."

He mentally crossed his fingers that she'd stay.

WENDY WOKE TO A VERY DARK ROOM, BUT THIS time, she heard movement in the shared bathroom. Zane was up, and she had a decision to make. Stay and work with horses or hide in a hotel. Seriously, when she phrased it that way, there was no consideration needed. She could think and reflect on her life while shoveling out stalls and riding horses. That'd be more pleasurable than staring at four walls all day.

She threw back the covers and stood. Yikes, the floor was cold on her bare feet. Warm bed covers beckoned her like chocolate. Stiffening her resolve, she remade her bed and got dressed. Later, as she walked downstairs for coffee, she found herself smiling and looking forward to the day, one thing that'd been missing from her life of late.

"Morning," she chirped as she walked down the stairs.

"Don't tell me. You're a morning person," Zane said with a loud sigh. "I hate morning people."

She laughed. "How can you grow up on a ranch and not be a morning person?"

"I've tried. Trust me. But leaving my warm bed on a cold, winter morning is tough."

She could only imagine. No, really, she could imagine being in his bed and not wanting to leave, cold morning or not.

As her cup of coffee brewed, she leaned on the counter. "Lucky for me, I have the early morning gene. If I were at home, I'd already be up and probably on the way to the hospital."

"Hospital?" He frowned. "This early? Why?"

"My staff knows I prefer to start my surgeries as early as possible." She pulled her mug to her mouth and took a long swallow. "I bribe the surgery staff monthly to keep on their good side and keep my surgery schedule like I like it. Crap. I need to call my office today and remind my nurse to send our usual Christmas goodies up there."

She stopped talking and studied the confused look on his face. "What?"

"You're a doctor? How did I not know this?"

"Um, yeah. Didn't your mom tell you?"

"I have no idea. Sometimes, she gets going on some long-winded story, and I kind of tune her out." He had the look of a kid caught with his hand in the cookie jar. "I know. That's horrible, right?"

She grinned. "Is there a kid in the world who hasn't tuned out a parent from time to time?"

"So what kind of doctor?"

"Plastic surgeon."

"Hmm." The timer on the stove went off. "Breakfast," he announced as though it was the best idea ever.

On the walk to the barn, he asked, "Can you take the west wing today? There's only five horses there."

"Sure. Muck, water, feed, and exercise?"

"Exactly." He stopped and touched her arm. Even though she wore multiple layers of clothing, including a heavy winter coat, his simple touch sent ripples down her spine. "I know I've said this, but thank you again for doing this."

"Seriously, I'm happy to help. I've kind of missed ranch work lately."

He laughed. "Oh, yeah. I can see how a high-powered surgeon would miss shoveling horse shit from a stall."

She gave him a playful shove. "If only you knew how much shit doctors put up with on a daily basis, you'd understand that at least with mucking stalls, you know you'll eventually get to the end of the crap. With hospital regulations, insurance, HMOs, governmental rules, and so forth, the crap just keeps coming." She grabbed his sleeve and pulled him toward the barn. "Come on. Let's go. Albert's waiting on me."

With a chuckle and grin that sent her heart racing again, he nodded, and they walked on.

With a backward wave, she walked away from him and made her way to the west wing, an appropriate designation for what were the fanciest facilities the ranch offered. She didn't know what the ranch charged for boarding, but she knew enough about horses to know this wing had to be the most expensive.

She probably should be flattered that he'd given her what she assumed were his highest paying clients. Then again, it made no difference to her. She loved all horses…even the sometimes-bitchy mares.

Albert greeted her with a toss of his head, and in her mind, a broad smile.

"Good morning, handsome," she said, opening the door to his palace. "You are looking quite fetching this morning." She scratched behind his ears as he butted her shoulder over and over.

"Right," she said. "Let's get to work."

She'd finished mucking the stalls when she heard voices echoing down the barn aisle.

"I promised her I'd introduce you two when you got here," she could hear Zane saying. "Be nice."

"Wendy? You got a minute? I want you to meet Sally Carter and Lynne Bailey."

Wendy prepared herself to meet two young, fit women. She expected their attention to be focused on the hunky cowboy more than a visiting ranch guest, but he did say he would bring them around, and apparently, he was a man of his word.

"Sure." She wiped the straw dust off her face and turned. What she saw wasn't what she'd expected at all.

Well, the Zane adoration was clear on their faces. She'd gotten that right, but that was about it.

"Hi," she said with a broad grin.

"This is Sally Carter and Lynne Bailey."

The two preteens smiled. "Hi," they said in unison.

"I'm Sally."

"I'm Lynne."

Sally was a cute blonde with a mouth full of braces. She was dressed in worn jeans, a flannel shirt, and dirty boots.

Lynne was a heavy-set brunette wearing a thick pair of glasses.

"Nice to meet you both," Wendy said. "Zane said you take care of your horses."

"We do," Sally said. "Either my mom or Lynne's mom drive us out here before school." She shrugged. "It was the deal we made so our parents would get us horses."

"Yeah," Lynne said. "I wish I could come every day."

"You want to live here," Sally said in a teasing, sing-song voice.

Lynne's cheeks pinked as she dipped her head to glance at Zane. "Do not," she muttered.

"Well, I sure do," Wendy said. "Who wouldn't want to live on a cool ranch like this?"

Lynne's gaze shifted to Wendy. "I guess it wouldn't be too bad."

Zane laughed. "All right you two. Back to work. You still have to get to school today."

"Bye," both called as they hurried back the way they'd come.

Wendy eyed Zane. "You knew I wasn't expecting a couple of cute pre-teens, didn't you?"

He grinned. "Maybe."

She laughed and pitched a fork of clean straw at him. "Go away. I still have work to do."

He threw up his hands. "I'm going. I'm going. But before I leave, do you need some help?"

"Nope. I'm good."

"Not too much?"

"Nope. I'd like to take Albert out for a ride in about an hour or so. That okay?"

"Sure. Make it ninety minutes and I should be able to shake myself free if you want company. Thought you might want to see the cabins Eli and I are working on."

"I'd love the company and I'd love to see that area. You've got yourself a date."

She regretted her words as soon as they left her mouth. She didn't want him to think she was asking him to take her on a date.

"I don't mean a *date* date," she rushed to add.

He gave a careless shrug. "I knew what you meant."

As soon as he was out of earshot, she scratched Albert's nose. "Argh. Be glad you're a horse. Being a person is so much work."

She was saddling Albert when Cowboy Russ sauntered up to the stall. "Hey, Wendy."

The young cowboy twitched and didn't meet her gaze. Something was going on.

"Hey, Russ. What's up?"

"Seeing if you need any help."

"I'm good."

"Great. Um, Zane sent me down to tell you he had to run to town and couldn't go with you riding."

Wendy nodded, a tug of disappointment in her chest. "No problem."

"I can go with you," Russ offered.

"You don't have to do that. I won't go far."

"Actually, Zane asked me to."

Wendy rolled her eyes. "Seriously, I'll be fine."

"Sure. No way to really get lost, but I need to exercise a couple of the horses, so if you don't mind the company…"

"I don't mind at all."

"Meet you in front of the main barn," Russ said.

She ended up spending the rest of the afternoon with Russ. The ranch hand was a nice guy who loved his job, loved his wife, and thrilled that they were expecting their first child in the spring. She tried to think of seemingly innocent questions to ask about Zane to get a better feel for her host, but in the end, she left the subject in the mud.

Later in the afternoon, she helped Russ bring in the horses that had been released into the pasture, "help" being a relative term. Her job was to open the pasture gate that crossed the drive. Russ handled the other side. Then he let go of a loud whistle.

The ranch dogs came running at the sound.

"Pike, come by. Coda, away."

At the commands, Pike took off to the left of the horse herd with Coda headed to the right. The two dogs circled around and began moving the horses toward the open gates. The herd picked up speed and trotted quickly through the gates and into the barn.

"Impressive," Wendy called, as she closed the gate.

Russ nodded. "Yelp. Always fun to watch. Thanks for the help today."

"Need me to help put the horses up?"

He shook his head. "Not this group. They all know exactly where they need to go and I suspect they are already in their stalls having dinner." He walked toward the barn with a wave.

"Home," he called to the dogs.

Pike and Coda bounded up to Wendy, their tongues lolling out of their mouths. They circled her, yapping and nipping at her boots.

"I got it," she said. "Dinner time for you guys too, right?"

They ran ahead of her but kept circling back to make sure she was following. She laughed at their antics as she scanned for Zane's truck. Russ had said he had to go to town and his truck was still missing.

At the house, since she wanted the company, she cleaned the dogs' feet in the outer mudroom area before removing her own muddy boots.

"Okay, okay," she said to the dogs as she opened the door. "Stay here and dry, and I promised to find you a treat."

When she strolled into the house, she was surprised to find Zane sitting in front of a roaring fire. The room was toasty warm, much like the heat that filled her chest when she noticed him.

"Hey," she said, coming to an abrupt stop.

"Hey, yourself." He turned to look at her, and damn if little tingles didn't flare in her gut. "Sorry to miss the ride."

She shrugged off his comment. "No biggie."

"Any problems?"

"None whatsoever."

"You look surprised to see me."

"I am. I didn't see your truck outside."

"Ah. Lori took it this morning. She had some errands to run, and since it's four-wheel drive and has snow tires, I made her take it." He frowned. "Why are you standing way over there?" He stood and pulled the other chair closer to the fire. "You have to be a few degrees from freezing."

"I was trying to decide what to do with the dogs. I left them in the entry room."

"I suspect they're muddy, right?" When she nodded, he said. "Leave them. They're fine. Let them dry some. Now come on and get warm."

"You're right. I am cold." Rather than sit, she stood in front of the fireplace and held her hands up to warm them. "Mmm," she hummed. "Much better."

"I wonder if you can help me with something for the next couple of days."

She turned toward him, letting the heat from the fire warm her frigid rear. "What do you need?"

He swept his hand around the room. "Don't you think this room lacks something?"

Her gaze moved around the area. "Actually, I like this room. So comfortable and homey." She looked at him. "Don't tell me you're thinking about new furniture. It'd be criminal to get rid of these comfy chairs."

Laughing, he shook his head. "Nope. Mom would strangle me if I did that. What I was thinking was there's no Christmas. I thought maybe you could help me drag out all Mom's decorations and surprise her when she and Dad get back."

"Oh? They're coming back for Christmas?"

"Supposed to. That's what my errand today was all about. Look out the back door."

She did as instructed and saw a large, almost perfect, blue spruce. "You got a Christmas tree."

"I did. So decorating? You in?"

Chapter Eight

As a general rule, Zane did not get nervous around women. Either they liked him or they didn't. If they didn't, no big deal. There'd be another woman soon enough who did.

As another general rule, he also never usually questioned that he was the smartest person in the room. He'd excelled in high school and college and graduated with honors from both. Getting his Master of Business Administration degree from the University of Chicago had been more endurance than intellectually demanding. His work as a financial advisor, investment banker, and then hedge fund manager had consumed his time, but not enthused him like working with animals and their at-times unpredictability did.

However, Wendy McCool was not just challenging both of these rules. She was destroying them like a flame torch to an ice cube. She confused and frustrated him. He couldn't say if she was attracted to him. He was attracted to her, which was why the whole situation drove him crazy and kept him awake at night. Plus, when sleep came, his dreams were filled with erotic sex acts and one sensual, blonde doctor.

The two days of Christmas decorating were interesting. Lots of Christmas carols were sung—badly on his part, passable on hers. Gallons of hot apple cider with a few beers thrown in kept them warm and happy. Stories from Christmases past were freely shared, and he wished he'd known her back then.

While he had a tendency to place all the holiday trimmings where his mother always had, Wendy moved everything, rearranging his placements to suit her vision for the decorations. He had to admit, she was usually right. She brought a new perspective and look to the house.

The tree, which was always in the corner, had been moved to the front window of the living room. The ornaments had been spread evenly around the tree as opposed to grouped toward the front. She had insisted on going into Gardiner for more energy efficient strands of Christmas lights and had surprised him by bringing home tinsel. He hadn't seen tinsel on a tree since he was a kid.

And after he told her about the old angel tree topper his family had passed down through the years, she'd insisted he search the attic until he found it. The poor doll had seen better days, but she'd sent him out on Friday to work with Russ while she cleaned and repaired the blonde angel.

Late Friday evening, he walked into the house and

came to a stunned stop. Small, white twinkling lights draped the fireplace mantle and every window. His mother's Christmas village had been arranged along the top of the mantle and each building shone with an internal bulb. The aroma of fresh cedar and apple cider scented the air and filled his senses. The lights on the tree blinked, making the tinsel sparkle. Under the tree were five wrapped gifts.

"Wow," he said. "Just wow." His gaze moved across everything she'd done until it landed on his grandparents' angel now perched on the top of the tree. A smile curved his lips as he walked over. "I can't believe you made her look so good." He looked over at her. "Thank you."

Her cheeks pinked, and she shrugged. "It was nothing. I enjoyed the challenge, although her hair is still a tad ragged."

"No, no, not at all. She's beautiful." He chuckled. "What is she wearing?" He stepped closer and looked up.

"Her gown was beyond repair, so I sewed her a new one but I have to be honest. The stitches are more surgical than dressmaker's."

He chuckled. "Where did you get that material? It looks like satin."

"I'm a little embarrassed to say. Can't you just enjoy how she looks and not ask too many questions?"

"I can and thank you. This deserves a dinner out, I believe."

She smiled, and his gut tugged, hard.

"Don't tell me that there are some fine dining establishments in the area."

"Depends on your definition of fine dining, I guess. Give me ten minutes to shower and change." He studied her jeans and flannel shirt. "For where I'm taking you, you're fine in what you're wearing."

He hoped she'd like the Old Saloon. He knew the gal singing there tonight, and she was good. Probably too good for such a small area, but her time for the big stage would come. He was sure of it.

Before Zane and Wendy left, Pike and Coda were fed and put into their kennels for the evening. Lori wasn't back in his truck, which was odd given it was after five, but she'd grown up in the area and could drive these roads as well as Zane. Now that he thought about it, she had mentioned doing some Christmas shopping in Bozeman after her doctor's appointment.

They got in his mom's Jeep and headed toward Highway 89, turning left when he reached it.

"Wait. Isn't Gardiner to our right? Or am I turned around?" Wendy asked.

"No, you're right but we aren't headed to Gardiner. We're going to the Old Saloon in Emigrant."

"Saloon."

He chuckled. "Trust me. It's a landmark in the area. Been here since the turn of the century."

"2000?"

With a laugh, he said, "No, the prior turn of the century. It was built around 1902 or so, and it's been there since, well, sort of. It burned down a few years after it was built, but there were so many cowboys and railroad people in the area that it was rebuilt quickly." He glanced over. "Missing out on the money, you know?"

"Got it."

"And then there was that nasty prohibition era, but my dad says that only moved the liquor sales to private, if you get my drift."

"Got it again."

"When my dad was a kid, the owner dragged a livery stable down and attached it to the bar, adding a real dining room."

"So we're eating in a livery stable?"

He looked over and laughed at the questioning expression on her face. "We could, but I've got a table reserved in the bar. So much more character in there, not to mention the people watching."

"You like to people watch?"

"Who doesn't? Don't you?"

"Oh, hell yeah. I thought it was more of a girl thing."

"I used to get so bored at those society functions I had to attend for business that my eyes would glaze over. People watching kept me awake."

"Society functions? In Gardiner?"

With a snort and then a laugh, he shook his head. "Good Lord, no. Chicago. The social events here are much better." He snapped his fingers. "I forgot to tell you. Since you're staying for a while, there is a pre-Christmas bonfire celebration at Two-Ton Ranch next Thursday. Love for you to go with me."

"Wait," she said, her eyes blinking rapidly. "I'm confused. Chicago? Society? We'll get to the bonfire, but Chicago? What are you talking about?"

His eyebrows drew down. "Chicago, as in Illinois. Until about six months ago, I lived there."

"You did? But...but the ranch?"

"My parents ran it. Remember I mentioned that my mother had been ill?" At her nod, he continued, "Cancer. I came back to help and realized I didn't want to go back, so I didn't."

"Honest to God, my head is spinning. You could knock me over with a feather."

He poked her shoulder with his index finger, and with a dramatic swoon, she fell against the passenger door. He laughed.

"What did you do?"

"Financial advising, then I got into investment banking, and finally hedge fund managing. I still manage the hedge fund, but from here instead of Chicago."

"You any good?"

He grinned at her. "I'm the best, doll, the best."

"Hmm. This is all very interesting and completely mind-blowing. I don't know why I just assumed you'd lived here all your life. Maybe it's the way you handle the ranch, like you've done it forever."

"Thanks. I appreciate that. Here we are," he said as they pulled into a dirt and gravel lot.

From the look of the building's exterior, the Old Saloon hadn't changed in decades. It still looked like an old-west building complete with hitching rail in the front. While there were no horses tonight, he'd been here when there were. He wished there'd been a couple tonight. That would have blown Wendy's mind.

"Well, you weren't kidding about the name," she said. "Looks pretty much as I'd pictured it in my mind."

"Bet you don't have anything like this in Dallas."

She smiled. "Some try to be, but nothing as authentic as this."

"I figured it would be busy tonight with Harley Queen providing the music," he said as he cruised the side lot looking for a parking spot. "I didn't quite expect the parking to be this bad yet."

"Harley Queen? That's her real name?"

"Yup. I've known Harley since first grade. Needless to say, she was addressed as Her Majesty as a joke. Ah, there's one," he said, swinging into a slot between a rusty ranch truck and a pair of muddy ATVs.

By the time he got around the car, she'd opened her door and was gliding out. He took her hand as she stood, then shut and locked the car. Once she was standing by him, he continued holding her hand as they walked through the snow and slush to the front. Her hands were covered with thick gloves, as any sane person's would be in these temperatures, but he missed the palm-to-palm, fingers-to-fingers, skin-to-skin contact. As he led her around to the front, she didn't try to pull her hand away, so he took that as a good sign.

Even though he'd told himself he wasn't looking to

start anything with her, he couldn't stem his growing attraction and admiration. At thirty-eight, he knew what he liked in a woman and she clicked every box. She was smart and funny, and damned if he didn't find himself getting home earlier every day just so he'd have more time in the evenings with her. He'd found his nights getting later as he'd prolonged their evenings and delayed heading to bed. Some nights, simply knowing she was across the hall made getting to sleep difficult.

They entered the bar, which was already getting crowded.

"Zane," the bartender called.

Zane gave a head nod toward the bar. "Hank. Good to see you, man."

"Edie and Frank are holding a table for you."

"Thanks."

"Edie and Frank?" she said into his ear.

Her warm breath on his neck sent his mind down an erotic path and it took a couple of seconds for him to respond.

"Friends," he finally got out, after swallowing against the lust bubbling up. "Remember I mentioned a bonfire? It's in a field on their ranch next Thursday. Thought you might like to know someone other than me, that is, if I can get you to go."

"I'd love to go, and I'm looking forward to meeting your friends."

He threaded them through the crowd, stopping now and then to speak with locals, never once releasing her hand.

"Zane. Over here."

He turned toward the voice and saw Edie waving from the booth under an antlered deer head.

"Hey, Edie." He bussed her cheek. "Frank, good to see you."

The two men shook hands.

"Wendy, this is my oldest friend, Frank Dale, and his wife, Edie. Guys, this is Dr. Wendy McCool."

"Nice to meet you," Edie said, extending her hand.

"You, too. Call me Wendy. And nice to meet you, too, Frank."

Frank shook her hand. "You are too pretty to be seen with this character," he said with a nod toward Zane. "And a doctor, too? Definitely too smart for him."

Zane groaned. "Thanks for all the help."

Frank slapped Zane's back. "What are friends for?"

Frank slid into the booth first, leaving Edie the outside seat. "Poor baby has to get up about every twenty minutes," he explained to Zane and Wendy as they slid in on their side.

"Hey," Edie said as she struggled to get her and her very pregnant belly back into the booth. "I didn't do this by myself, buster."

Wendy laughed. "When are you due?"

"Not soon enough," Edie said with a groan.

"First?"

"Second. We have a two-year-old son at home, or

rather with Frank's folks tonight. Social services frowns on leaving two-year-olds home alone."

Wendy chuckled.

Frank wrapped his arm around his wife. "It's date night," he said with a pump of his eyebrows. "You know what that means?"

"Yeah," Edie said. "I get to go to sleep early and sleep late. The evidence of our last date night is fairly obvious."

Over drinks and dinner, Zane and Frank talked about ranching and trucks and the NCAA championship game in January. It was a challenge, but at the same time, Zane kept an ear on the women's discussion. He wanted Wendy to like his friends. He wasn't sure why that was so important to him, but it was.

When Harley Queen took the stage, Wendy twisted in her seat to look toward the music. She leaned her back against his chest, her hand resting on his thigh. His pulse rocketed and his cock took notice. He closed his eyes to try—in vain—to get the tsunami of lust under control. When he opened his eyes, Frank was staring at him.

Frank widened his eyes and tilted his head toward Wendy. "I like her." he mouthed.

Zane grinned. "Me, too."

"Sexy and gorgeous," Frank mouthed and then hung his tongue out of the corner of his mouth and panted.

His wife poked him in the ribs with her elbow and gave him the look every mother knows how to use to stop whatever is going on.

"She's great," Wendy said, over her shoulder.

"Yeah, she is," Zane replied, not sure if he was talking about the musician or the woman leaning on him.

For about five seconds, he pondered over the fact that this was not the right time to get involved, she was a rebound bride, and, worst of all, she lived in another state, and he had no intention of ever leaving Montana again.

Then she squeezed his knee. He looked down at her trim fingers on his jeans and, that was the last thought he had.

In the truck on the way home, Wendy hummed along with the music on the country radio station, her head rocking back and forth in time with the songs.

"Hey, I really liked your friends," she said.

"And they liked you."

"Think so?"

"I know so. The good thing about Edie is that if she likes you, you know. Of course, the bad thing about her is if she doesn't like you, you'll know that, too."

She laughed. "I like a person who lets you know where you stand, don't you?"

"I do."

Now he only had to decide if they were talking about each other or in general.

As they neared the ranch, snow began dumping on them. His visibility was cut to less than ten feet and he slowed the SUV to a crawl.

"We'll be fine," he assured her. "I could drive the rest of the way home with my eyes shut."

"Please don't."

He glanced over to determine if she was serious or nervous, but what he got was a huge grin and then a laugh.

"I trust your driving, Zane. Besides, we could probably walk from here if we had to. Of course, we'd be frozen stiff by the time we climbed the steps to the house."

"Yeah, well, I like my digits and dangly parts, so no thank you on walking."

She gasped and snorted. "Dangly parts?" She laughed from deep in her gut, which suckered punched him right in his.

He grinned and turned into the drive.

"You going straight to bed?" he asked.

"Not if you've got something better in mind."

Oh, he had better things in mind, but he decided he take it slower if he didn't want to run her out of his house and off to a hotel.

"Yeah. Come on in and I'll make you a brown bear."

She slid from the Jeep and met him at the hood as he walked around. "Brown bear?"

"It's a drink. Oh, I didn't ask you if you like chocolate."

She looked at him like he'd announced he was from Mars. "I'm going to assume that was a joke. Of course, I love chocolate."

"Great."

He took her gloved hand—damn gloves—and walked her to the door.

"Before we go in…" he said. "I'm wondering about something."

"Yeah? What's that?"

"What your mouth tastes like before chocolate."

He released her hand and shucked his gloves, stashing them in his coat pocket. Then he cupped her face in his fingers, his thumb stroking her bottom lip. Their gazes met and held as though he was giving her the opportunity to back away and put some distance between them. He might hold her face in his hands, but the permission for a kiss was in hers.

His gaze dropped to her mouth. He was going to kiss her, or at least she wanted him to. She'd been thinking about kissing him all evening. Had been wondering if he was a good kisser. Her mind had tried to envision the moves beyond kissing, but she wouldn't let herself go there.

Still, when she'd turned to watch the singer perform, she'd casually rested her hand on his thigh in an attempt to gage his reaction. She hadn't been disappointed. Beneath her palm, his muscles had twitched and jumped at her touch. When he'd put his hand over hers, every muscle in her body had twitched and jumped, too.

As the evening progressed, when he'd wanted to tell her something, he'd pull her tighter and whisper into her ear. His deep voice and those soft words had her twisting in her seat as chills and shivers ran through her from her head to her toes. Parts of her that had been dormant for years woke and stretched and wanted to be petted.

In the end, she didn't wait for him to make the first move. She flicked out her tongue and touched the tip to his thumb. His eyes darkened, and he pulled her to him. Their cold lips met in a sizzling-hot kiss. When he pulled back, she licked her bottom lip, wanting to capture his taste again.

"Get your answer?" she asked.

"Oh, yeah."

ONCE INSIDE, HE LET THE DOGS OUT TO RUN. SHE excused herself and rushed upstairs with a, "Be right back," tossed over her shoulder. She wanted to get out of these tight jeans and into something looser. But more importantly, she wanted to brush her teeth. Her cowboy burger and onion rings had been delicious, but she worried about the residue scent on her breath.

After getting her teeth so clean they squeaked, she slipped into black leggings, a pair of thick socks, and a T-shirt. At the last moment, she grabbed a long-sleeved flannel shirt and put it on. It was long enough to cover her ass, which she'd never thought was one of her best features. She slipped on her Ugg slippers with the warm, sheepskin lining and headed downstairs to try a brown bear.

She was looking forward to tasting the drink…first from the mug and then from Zane's mouth.

Zane was leaning over the hearth putting fresh logs on the fire. He still had on his dress jeans, a pair that displayed his firm butt in all its glory. The sleeves on his cotton oxford shirt were rolled up to mid-forearms. She'd never thought of forearms as yummy, but his made her mouth water.

His phone rang before she could say anything. He looked at the caller ID and answered.

"Hey, Priscilla. How you doing?"

He listened for a moment and then said, "I know. Me too. Of course, I miss you. This will be our first Christmas apart in what? Three years?"

Her heart skipped a beat. Her stomach dropped to her knees. There was no way she was getting involved in some love triangle. After the Roy fiasco at Mae's wedding, the last thing she needed was some guy with a girlfriend.

She crept back up the stairs, trying hard to not alert him to her presence. Once she reached the landing, she called down, "Zane? I'll see you in the morning. I'm hitting the rack."

She could hear him say, "Just a minute," and then, "Are you sure? I've got a nice fire going."

"I'm sure. Night."

Yeah, she was sure. She had no intention of joining the Zane Miller dating team.

Chapter Nine

For the next seven days, she didn't avoid Zane, but she didn't go out of her way to engage him. The wall around her heart was securely back in place. After all, he'd only been able to knock out a few chunks of one side of her self-preservation fortification. The phone call she'd overheard had cemented those holes in a hurry.

Every day, she got her work done and then found a horse that needed some exercise. There were a couple of days she took as many as three different horses out. Russ was thrilled to get done early and home to Lori.

As the week progressed, she met the other horse owners who came to help with the animal upkeep. All of them were individuals more interested in the horses than in grabbing Zane's eye or his ass. Color her surprised. What was wrong with the women in this area? A delicious cowboy right at their doorstep and not one of them was taking advantage of the situation. Blindness and insanity must be in the local water.

On the other hand, it was quite possible the women in this area knew him better than she did. Maybe he'd been a player his whole life and she was the only one foolish enough to be taken in by his charm.

Wednesday evening, Edie called her on the ranch phone. She wanted to make sure Wendy knew she was invited to tomorrow night's bonfire and hoped that Wendy would come.

Wendy told her she remembered and she was looking forward to it. It wasn't Edie's fault that Zane had a hidden girlfriend.

At breakfast on Thursday, Zane said, "You still up for the bonfire tonight?"

"Of course," she said. "I'm looking forward to it. It's been years since I've been to one." She smiled as memories from her past flashed through her head. "When I was in high school, we'd have a huge fire and pep rally before the football homecoming game." She laughed. "There were lots of items thrown into that fire to burn. One year, the quarterback and his date got into an argument and she threw his letterman's jacket into the flames."

He grinned. "That was you, wasn't it?"

She lifted her coffee mug to her mouth with a shrug. "Maybe. I refuse to answer, because I don't think the statute of limitations is up yet."

Pointing his mug at her, he said, "Remind me not to get on your bad side."

She pointed her mug back at him. "You remember that, buddy."

With that, she finished her coffee and headed out to the barn. She was sure she could stay busy until it was time to leave for the party. Besides, apparently Zane hadn't even realized she was avoiding him. She wasn't exactly doing that, but still, he hadn't even noticed something was bugging her.

There had been only that one kiss. A freaking, knee-weakening, panty-melting kiss, but still, just the one. He'd been a total gentleman all week.

Not that she wanted to admit it, but maybe she was overreacting. After all, she'd given Roy a quick kiss on the cheek, and look how that had been misinterpreted. She'd meant absolutely nothing romantic then and yet, Roy had taken that one situation and blown it completely out of proportion.

Maybe what had been a drop-dead, fantastic kiss for her had been just a so-so kiss for him. Holy cow. Was she a bad kisser? Now that was a horrible thought. No man she'd ever dated—or kissed— had complained. But then again, telling someone they needed to work on their kissing technique might be a tad too much for most people.

If she was going to stay here until at least the end of the year, she needed to grow up. Even if Zane made her feel like a teenager with her first crush, she shouldn't act like one. It was one kiss between mature adults with no promises.

That evening, before they got going, she helped him load the truck bed with chairs and beer.

"The essentials," he said as he slammed the truck gate.

She laughed. "Beer is essential?"

"Duh. And by the way, I didn't wear my high school letterman jacket tonight. I know better than trust you around a big fire."

She laughed. "I promised to behave." She dragged her fingers across her chest in an X. "Cross my heart."

He started the truck.

"What about the food?" she asked. "All the beer and no food could make for a very drunk Wendy."

He grinned, and the truck rolled forward. "Not to worry. We all pitch in money for the food. It's already there. Sheila and Cliff Lancaster own the local grocery and always provide what we need."

"That's convenient. We're headed to Edie and Frank's ranch?"

"Yup. The Two-Ton. He and his brother started this cattle ranch about fifteen years ago."

After a short fifteen-minute drive, Zane turned on a frozen dirt road and continued another mile or so before he parked among eight other dirty trucks.

As soon as she got out, she heard her name. "Wendy. Over here."

She saw Edie waving her hands to get her attention. She waved back and grabbed the two camp chairs from the back of the truck and headed over. Zane followed behind carrying the beer.

Zane opened the chairs and set one next to Edie.

"I'm so glad you came," Edie said. "I wasn't sure if bonfires were your thing."

"Are you kidding? This is great. How did you arrange such fantastic weather?"

There had been no snow or sleet or rain in the past three days. Instead, there had been sunshine. Granted, it was as cold as standing naked in a meat locker, but at least the ground wasn't too sloppy.

Edie grinned. "I think God felt sorry for me and is trying to make it up to me." When Wendy frowned, Edie added, "You know, pregnant at Christmas, peeing every twenty minutes, backaches, insomnia, swollen ankles, gas, and a long list of other delightful physical side effects. I hate that I have to drive to Bozeman to see my doctor. All those pee stops make driving to Bozeman a real pain in the, well, patootie."

Wendy laughed. "Poor girl."

Edie winced.

"What's wrong? You look in pain." Wendy leaned over and touched Edie's arm. "Are you okay?"

"Damn Braxton Hicks contractions." Edie rubbed her protruding belly.

"Are you sure they're just Braxton Hicks? Could they be labor pains?"

"Nope. Too early. Braxton...Ouch. That was a dozy."

Zane had wandered off to speak to the other party goers and was now being pulled by a large older woman back to where she and Edie sat.

"Wendy. Sheila wants to meet you."

The woman—Sheila, Wendy assumed—slugged Zane's shoulder. "Nice intro." She leaned over and held out her hand. "Sheila Lancaster."

Wendy took her hand and stood. "Nice to meet you. Wendy McCool."

"I hear you're a doctor."

Wendy smiled and nodded. "You heard correctly."

"Any chance you're looking to relocate? We sure could use a doctor closer than Livingston or Bozeman."

She laughed. "I'm not, no. I have a thriving practice in Dallas. This is just a little vacation from my life."

"Well, darn," Sheila said while snapping her gloved fingers. "I was hoping Zane here was using his charms to talk you into staying."

"Nope. No charming me to stay."

Sheila turned toward Zane and waited until he got his beer to his mouth. "Damn, Zane. I had high hopes for you. I'm so disappointed."

Zane choked on the beer and coughed. "What are you talking about? I told you she was only here for a couple of months."

Sheila waved him off. "Go away and let me gossip for a while." She grabbed the arms of his chair and pulled it closer to where Edie and Wendy sat.

He threw his hands up in the air. "I know when I'm not wanted."

The three women chuckled as he walked away and over to a group of men.

"So, are you the Sheila who owns the grocery store and provided the supplies for tonight?"

"Guilty as charged," she replied.

"She and Cliff have the only grocery store in

town, so don't get on their bad side," Edie said in a stage whisper. "You'll get the old veggies and worst cuts of meat."

Wendy laughed. "Got it. Well, if no one said so, it's very nice of you to take charge of the food."

Sheila patted her ample stomach. "I'm a gal who loves to eat, so trust me when I say something tastes good."

"How's the toy drive going this year?" Edie asked.

"Toy drive?" Wendy asked.

"Every year, Sheila and Cliff do a toy drive to make sure every child in the area gets something from Santa."

"That's so nice," Wendy said.

Sheila shrugged. "Frank and I both grew up poor. Neither of our families had a dime to spare, so when I say we had nothing, I'm not talking figuratively. We didn't have anything. Most of the time, it didn't bother me so much, but Christmas? That was hard. Both sets of parents did their best to provide, but back then, there just wasn't much work. We swore that our children would always have a Christmas to remember."

Wendy smiled. "So that's what you did? Went all out for Christmas for your kids?"

Sheila smiled, but it was a sad smile. "Sadly, no. Frank and I weren't able to have children of our own."

Wendy leaned forward and placed her hand over Sheila's. "I'm so sorry. I wouldn't have said anything if I'd had any idea."

Sheila placed her free hand over Wendy's, trapping her gloved hand between her own two. "Don't worry about it. How could you have known? We've adjusted. We have a great life together, but we want to do what we can for the less privileged in the area."

"They've done a toy drive for years," Edie said. "People can either give new toys still in the box or donate money. How's it going this year?"

Sheila shook her head. "Tough year. Lots of folks are suffering. Those who can give do, but I swear, it gets harder every year to cover all the kids."

"How short are we?" Edie asked. "I can get Frank to kick in a little more."

Wendy noticed Edie's use of the "we" and she liked that the young mother was trying to help others even though Wendy knew cattle prices were down and hay prices were up.

"It's bad, but you and Frank have done your share. You've got your own son to take care of, not to mention the new one coming. But I can't remember a year when there were so many needy children. We're down in financial contributions by close to two thousand. We have some toys already donated, but not nearly enough."

"Maybe others will step up to the plate as it gets closer to Christmas," Edie said.

"Maybe," Sheila replied with a shrug. "But with Christmas only four days away, I can only pray for a Christmas miracle."

"Good luck," Wendy said, her mind racing with ways she might help.

"Let's talk about something more fun," Edie said.

"Okay, let's," Sheila said. Her gaze swung from

Edie to Wendy. "Are you and the hot cowboy a thing? I bet he's as good in bed as he is on a horse, right?"

Wendy blinked rapidly. "I don't know what you're talking about."

"Please," Edie said, nudging Wendy's shoulder with the palm of her hand. "You think I didn't see how Zane was looking at you at dinner?"

"What? How?" Sheila leaned forward. "Tell me more. Let the old married woman live vicariously through you."

"I have no idea what Edie's talking about," Wendy said. "We're friends."

"Not hardly," Edie said with a scoff. She looked at Sheila. "He was looking at her like she was what he wanted for dinner instead of his twenty-eight-ounce strip steak."

"He was not," Wendy protested.

"Not when you were looking, but when you weren't? Whew! The temperature in that booth went up twenty degrees. Frank came home all frisky last Friday night from all the sexual tension over dinner."

Wendy laughed. "Frisky, huh? Well, that's not me and Zane, no matter what you think you saw. He has a girlfriend."

"No, he doesn't," Edie said.

"Sure he does. I heard him talking to her on the phone. Priscilla somebody."

Edie looked at Sheila, and both of them groaned.

"Priscilla Roth," Edie said. "That's over. Dead and buried."

Wendy shrugged. "Maybe, maybe not. Didn't

sound like it, but to be honest, I only heard a snippet. I didn't hang around to listen to their whole conversation."

"I can understand that you're a little gun shy about guys," Edie said. "I mean, diving back into dating after…Well, after that ass left you at the altar, but Zane's a good guy. He'd never hurt you like that."

"Wait. What?" Wendy's mouth gaped.

"Now, don't get mad at Zane for telling Frank," Edie said. "It's not your fault that your groom fell in love with your maid of honor."

"That's right, honey," Sheila said, reaching over to squeeze Wendy's hand. "Not your fault at all."

Wendy put her elbows on her knees and held her head in her hands. "Oh dear God," she muttered.

"Nothing to be embarrassed about," Edie said, patting her back.

"No, you don't understand. I wasn't the jilted bride. My cousin was." She sighed. "I was the maid of honor."

Edie's mouth dropped, and then she covered it with her hand. "Oh dear."

"Oh dear is right. It was horrible."

"What happened?" Sheila asked.

"First, you have to understand that I adore my cousin Mae. She's like a little sister to me. She and Roy—that was the groom—are a few years younger than I am. I knew the groom's older brother. He traveled for his job…a lot. I wanted Roy and Mae to have the perfect wedding, so I stepped in to do some of the best-man duties in addition to the maid-of-honor stuff I had to do. I took Roy to get his hair cut, to get his tux fitted, even planned the bachelor party. He totally misinterpreted my help." She shrugged. "Or maybe he got cold feet, and I was an easy out for him. I don't know. All I do know is that Mae was horribly hurt, and Roy was lucky to leave with his balls intact."

Sheila slapped her forehead. "Oh my goodness. I saw this on one of the Sunday morning shows. What was it? Two months ago?"

Wendy nodded. "Sadly, yes. Someone had their phone out and taped the whole thing. Both families were terribly embarrassed."

"How's your cousin doing?" Edie asked

"Okay. Threw herself back into work, which is what we all expected. She'll be fine."

"Better to be embarrassed at the altar than go through some long, drawn-out divorce."

"It's easy to look at the whole event and see that, but at the time, I kept wanting to wake up from that bad dream."

Edie frowned. "Does Zane know this story?"

"We've never discussed it, but I assume his mother explained why I needed to get away from Dallas." She shook her head. "I just needed a break."

Edie burst out laughing, rocking in her chair. "Help me up, help me up," she said, still laughing. "I'm going to wet myself if I don't get to the bathroom."

Wendy and Sheila leapt to their feet to pull Edie up.

"Why are you laughing so hard?" Wendy asked as they walked toward the house.

"Honey, Zane thinks you're the jilted bride, so he's trying to be thoughtful and considerate. Otherwise, he'd be jumping your bones like you were a mare in heat."

Even though the night was frigid, heat rushed to Wendy's face. "No way. He's just being a gentleman and good host."

Sheila laughed and threw an arm around Wendy's shoulders. "Oh, honey. Zane is not a nice gentleman. Well, he's nice and a gentleman, but if Edie is being honest about how he was eyeing you last Friday, you have definitely caught his attention. Trust me when I say Zane Miller goes after what he wants, and if what he wants is you and he's holding back, it can only be because he's trying to get close without spooking you, like he would a skittish mare." Sheila cackled. "Well, this is interesting."

Wendy's lips tingled at the thought of last week's kiss. She hated to admit how weak she was around him, but yeah, she might not have stopped with just a kiss last Friday night had there not been that over-heard phone call.

At the memory of that call, her heart shrank to the size of a peanut. "And so we now circle back to Priscilla. He told her he missed her. His voice was so caring."

Edie stopped and looked at her. "Trust me. He talks to Frank. They're like two old women gossiping all the time. He's trying to get Priscilla to either buy his condo in Chicago or move out. I met her once when we went there to visit Zane. She is a royal bitch. She is the center of her world and thinks everyone else should see how important she is. She isn't, by the way. Having rich parents gave her such a sense of entitlement. And her temper?" Edie dramatically rolled her eyes. "I saw it in person. Ever seen a two-year-old throw a temper tantrum? Yeah, like that. Zane was embarrassed and kept apologizing for her, saying she'd had a tough week. I wanted to ask what could have been tough for her?"

Wendy shrugged. "Maybe she'd had a bad week at work?"

Edie laughed. "She's the vice president of social media at her daddy's law firm. I think she has a staff of three assistants."

Sheila guffawed. "Good lord. Works hard, doesn't she?"

"During the week we were there, I never saw her go into the office. Not once. Didn't even call and check in. She was too busy holding on to Zane's arm like she was afraid to let him out of her sight, like maybe Frank and I were there to lure him back to Montana."

They arrived at Edie and Frank's house and went in the back door. "Be right back," Edie said and rushed off.

"While we're alone, I wanted to tell you that I'd like to help out with your toy project," Wendy told Sheila.

"You don't have to," Sheila replied. "But I would never turn down help."

"I'll come by your store tomorrow, if that's okay? I want to keep this between us."

"Sure. I'm good with secrets." The older woman grinned. "Especially if they benefit me."

Later, on the drive back to the Grizzly Bitterroot Ranch, Wendy asked Zane about the toy drive.

"Cliff and Sheila are good people," he said. "They're about twenty years older than me, I think. I kind of remember hearing Mom talk about their inability to have a family. At the time, I was more concerned with *not* getting some girl pregnant, so my sympathies for their situation might have been quite reserved. But as I've gotten older and seen Frank with his son and the joy it brings him, I've developed more of a soft spot for what Cliff and Sheila must have gone through. I have great respect for how they used their tragedy to motivate themselves and the community to help needy families in the area."

His comments about children and family made her wonder if he was feeling his biological clock ticking. Not that a guy had the same type of biological clock as a woman. He could father children for decades.

She, on the other hand, was thirty-five. Her biological clock wasn't just ticking. It was bonging like Big Ben at midnight.

Did she want children? She couldn't have answered that question if someone had put a gun to her head.

The love she felt for her nephew was more than she'd thought possible. She loved her sister. Loved her family. But with her having so many doubts and questions about her life—professional as well as personal—the idea of a husband and child was nebulous in her mind.

Here at the Grizzly Bitterroot, she could barely stay awake long enough to shower before dropping into bed with exhaustion. But her tiredness was a different kind of tired than she'd had at home. In Dallas, at the end of the day, she was tired, but in an itchy sort of way, as though she could have gotten more done if she'd been more organized. Not here in Montana. She slept every night with a satisfied smile.

"So why did you ask about the toy drive?"

Zane's question pulled her from her musings.

"Oh, no reason. Sheila mentioned that donations were down this year."

"And you're wondering if I've donated? Well, the answer is yes. My family has always supported their event. I do, too. I started supporting their toy drive as soon as I had a dollar I could give. But if they need help this year, they should've put the word out. People would have scrapped together what they could have."

"I know. This town seems like that kind of place, but she didn't want to stress the finances of families already stretched this year."

She thought about telling him that she was meeting with Sheila tomorrow to see what she could do, but in the end, she decided against it. He might object or tell her this project was for the locals, and she didn't need to get involved. And nobody told her what she should, or shouldn't do.

"Are you going home for Christmas?" he asked. "We haven't talked about it."

"I don't know yet, is that okay? I can still move to a hotel if I'm in the way at all for your family's holiday."

"Eli isn't coming home. I talked to Mom earlier today, and Dad isn't feeling well, so they are holding off on making a travel decision until they know more."

He looked over at her and then dropped his hand on hers and squeezed. The touch might have been on her hand, but the pressure was felt deep in her heart. She had mixed emotions about how she felt about that.

"I'd love for you to stay," he continued. "The horses don't know it's Christmas, and they still want to be fed and watered…those greedy heathens."

She laughed. "Horses. Sheesh. They think we are here to serve them."

"Especially Albert."

"You know it," she said with a chuckle. "But he's really a good horse."

"He is." He put his hand back on the truck's steering wheel. "Then it's settled. You'll stay."

"I'll check with my family and let you know."

"Okay, but think how lonely Albert will be if you're not here."

She snorted.

Chapter Ten

"Hey, I need to borrow the truck," she said over coffee the next morning. "I've got some errands to run. Is that okay?"

"Sure," he said. "Drive the Jeep. Mom said it needs to be driven while she's away. Anything I can help you with?"

"Nope. Secret girl stuff."

He held up his hands in surrender. "Say no more. I ask no questions." He pulled a set of keys off a wall holder and tossed them to her. "Here ya go."

She caught them. "Thanks."

"How long will you be gone?"

She shrugged. "Don't know. Don't expect me until you see me."

"So, in other words, you're ditching work today."

"Yup. You have to make do without me, but..."
She opened the refrigerator and pulled out a bag of

carrots. "These are for the west wing. The big one is for Albert."

"No wonder those guys are always glad to see you." He downed the last swallow of coffee and put the mug in the dishwasher. "Have fun. See you when I see you."

Now that he was gone, she had a few things she needed to do, like laundry.

At eight, she pulled into Gardiner Market and parked. This being the last shopping weekend before Christmas, the store was packed with customers on every aisle. Checkout lanes beeped with sales. She found Sheila in a small office near the front of the store.

"Good morning," Wendy said. "Looks crazy busy."

"It is," Sheila said. "Now, what can I do for you?"

"You can let me help with the toy drive. Can you explain what you do? Maybe I can see where I can pitch in."

"We hold a party at the community center on Christmas Eve. The day before, we decorate it to the nines. The families come for dinner, and then Santa arrives to give out presents. I try the best I can to get with the parents ahead of time to make sure every child gets some quote unquote big present. It might be a bike, or ice skates, or something like that. It depends on the age of the child."

"How do you identify families in need?"

"Wendy, I could throw a dart with my eyes shut and hit a needy family."

"That's awful. I want to help. I can write you a check, buy some toys, or do whatever you need. Just say the word, only I don't want others to know."

Sheila tapped her chin. "Of course, I can keep it quiet. That's not a problem. But honestly, anything you do will help."

"Let's start with the toys. How are you fixed there?"

"I'm going shopping this afternoon in Bozeman. Want to come?"

Wendy grinned. "I would love to."

By the time Wendy rolled back onto the ranch, it was close to nine p.m. She'd only thought she was young and spry. Sheila had outshopped and outwalked her all day, but their shopping trip had been successful. The Lancasters' large van was stuffed with bikes, dolls, games, books, puzzles and a variety of toys based on Sheila's list. Wendy hadn't blinked as she'd written out a two-thousand-dollar check to cover their purchases and would have been happy to have written a larger one if needed.

Pike and Coda met her at the door, both demanding a minute, or ten, of belly rubs and kisses. The Christmas tree lights flashed on and off in the corner. The white lights woven into the greenery on the mantle twinkled. Hot flames from the fireplace warmed the room, both the temperature and the atmosphere. All the scene needed to be a Hallmark movie was mistletoe and a hot guy. Check. There he was.

Zane was sprawled on the sofa by the fireplace

watching college basketball. He muted the sound and sat up when she entered.

"Worried I ran off with your mom's car?"

He chuckled. "Nope. I knew exactly where it was. Cliff called me this afternoon about a grocery order. Told me you were off with Sheila." He narrowed his eyes. "What were you two up to? Cliff said you were as thick as thieves and as closed-mouthed as a virgin's first kiss about where you were headed."

She snorted. "As closed-mouthed as a virgin's first kiss? Now that's funny." She bent down to nuzzle Coda's nose with her cheek.

"Have you eaten?" He stood and started toward the kitchen. "There's some leftover pizza."

"I'm good. Sit back down. I've been here long enough that you don't have to wait on me. If I were hungry, I'd head into the kitchen and make something."

He dropped back onto the sofa. "There's beer."

She pointed at him. "Now that's what I'm talking about. Be right back."

She brought a couple of beers back to the living room.

"For me?" he asked with a grin that took her breath away.

"Nope. Both are for me."

He sighed loudly, and she handed over one of the bottles.

A slightly lopsided grin tugged at his lips. "I knew you liked me."

With a roll of her eyes, she sat in her usual chair. "What did I miss today around here?"

"Not at thing. Albert's mad, so you might have to baby him a little tomorrow."

"What did you do?"

He held up his hands. "Nothing. I swear. He just likes you better than me."

"What can I say? I'm charming like that."

"Yes, you are." All joking was gone from his voice, and his eyes darkened. "What did you do today?" he asked on a lighter note. "I'm thinking it was something to do with Sheila and Cliff's toy drive. That's about the only thing that would get her out of the store the Friday before Christmas."

She took a long draw of beer and set the bottle on the table. "Fine, but I don't want others around here to know. I helped her finish up her toy shopping and got everything wrapped and tagged for the party."

"That was nice of you."

She shrugged. "I can afford it, so why not? One of the reasons I'm a doctor is to help people."

As the words left her mouth, she felt the truth in them. She was a good doctor, and she did help people. She hadn't felt this optimistic about her future in medicine in a long time. And as much as she loved animals, their pain and suffering was more than she could tolerate. With people, at least she could talk to them and find out what hurt. So maybe medicine was her path after all, but she still wasn't convinced plastics was her calling.

"Are you missing your old life? Missing your patients?"

"Yes and no. But I am glad to be here right now."

"And I'm glad you're here. Tonight reminded me how quiet and empty the house is when I'm here alone."

"You didn't live alone in Chicago?"

Yup, she was digging for information on the man, so sue her.

"Officially, yes. The last couple of years, I had a girlfriend who was there a lot. Not exactly living together, but she seemed to spend more time there than at her own place." Their gazes met. "She's still there, but we ended before I moved home."

"Ah." Wendy nodded and took another swallow of beer. The frigid liquid slid down her throat and splashed into her empty stomach. She waited for him to add to his backstory, but he changed the subject instead.

"I talked to my parents today. Dad's running a fever. The doctor says it's the flu and he is confined to bed until after Christmas, so they won't be coming. It's just you and me this year, if you've decided to stay."

"Oh, no. I'm sorry. Not about Christmas being just us two," she hurried to add. "I mean your dad. The flu bug this year has been wicked."

"Let's hope it stays away from here."

"Agreed."

"I told Mom not to worry about them not making it home, that you would be here, so I wouldn't be alone. You *are* going to stay, right?"

"Sure. I'll call home and let the folks know." She checked the time. "But not tonight. It's too late to call, but I will. Since I won't need Dad's plane to pick me up, and, as far as I know the rest of the family is staying put, the crew will get the holidays off. I'm sure they'll like it. Are you giving Russ and Lori the day off, too?"

"If you weren't here to help, I couldn't. I don't think I could get everything done. But with your help, sure. Besides, it's their last Christmas together as a couple before the baby comes and everything changes."

Man, she felt like she was surrounded by babies. Her sister, then Edie, and now Lori. Was the universe trying to tell her something?

"It'll be a busy day for sure."

"Want to go to the community center tomorrow and help decorate for Christmas Eve? Cliff mentioned something today about needing another pair of hands."

"I'm ahead of you. I already told Sheila I'd be there." She stood and stretched. "And on that note, I'm going to bed. I'll see you in the morning."

She made it as far as the first step before he called her name. She stopped and waited for him to catch up.

"Yes?"

"Thank you," he said, and snaked his hand behind her neck to pull her closer...*For a kiss?*

She was right.

This time, his lips were warm and full as their

mouths pressed together. The tip of his tongue traced the loose seam between her lips, and she opened, allowing him to thrust inside. He tasted of beer and male yumminess.

In response, her heart galloped while her knees softened like butter in a microwave. She shuffled her feet to the edge of the step and grabbed handfuls of his shirt, pulling him closer.

He pulled away long enough to change the angle of his head and take her mouth again in a searing kiss of deep tongue thrusts.

She moaned deep in her throat. Her panties dampened with the melting of her center…And her resistance.

She wrapped her arms around his neck and pressed her aching, swollen breasts against his chest. God, she wanted to drag this man to her room, strip him, and run her tongue from his mouth all the way down to his toes, and then start all over again.

As good as touching him felt, and as much as she craved his touch, she had to stop this now. Regardless of what Edie and Sheila had assured her about Priscilla, she wasn't one-hundred percent clear about Zane's availability. Not that she was looking for a commitment, but if there was still something— anything—between this woman in Chicago and him, she didn't want to be a side in another triangle.

She pushed back and drew in a deep, calming breath. Yeah, that didn't help. Her heart continued to race and pound in her ears. Her choppy breaths spoke volumes. She swallowed the lust rock in her throat.

She looked at him. His eyes were black pools of lust and desire and she suspected hers were much the same. His chest heaved with his ragged breaths. She traced a fingertip down his cheek and across his wet lips. She really wanted this man in her arms and her bed.

She took a step back. "I…I better go to bed, erm, get some sleep." She produced a fake yawn and stretched. "Good night, Zane."

She looked over her shoulder and found him watching her, his expression as disappointed as she felt. At their ages, neither was inexperienced in life or sex. If there were no other lovers in either of their lives to be hurt by infidelity, maybe she should let things take the natural course when two healthy adults desired each other…to the bedroom.

"Sweet dreams," he said, his voice thick and husky.

Sweet dreams, her ass. If she could even get to sleep after that kiss, she suspected her dreams would be starring a dark-haired cowboy doing incredibly erotic things to her.

The next morning, she stumbled downstairs, her eyes still half-closed. A glance at the clock on the stove showed she'd slept to almost seven.

"Good morning," she muttered as she passed him sitting on a barstool on her way to the coffee pot.

"Good morning." His voice was deep with morning huskiness and a little too chipper for her liking. "Sleep good?"

She hoped he'd slept as little as she had. And those

sweet dreams he'd wished her? Not hardly. If she'd gotten three hours of sleep, she'd be surprised. But she'd gotten by on less.

"Slept like a rock," she lied. "You?"

"Great," he said, as though announcing the winning number in a lottery ball drawing. "Best night I've had in a while."

"Super," she said into her mug. She took a big gulp of her caffeine. "I think I want some breakfast. You hungry?"

He shook his head. "I've already eaten. I woke up at four and got some work done. I'm going to head out and help Russ finish early. We need to leave for the community center by three, if not earlier. You're still game to help decorate, right?"

"Yes." She propped an elbow on the counter and held her head in her hands.

"You look exhausted," he said.

"Gee, thanks. Just what every woman wants to hear."

He laughed. "I didn't mean it that way. You had a hard day yesterday. Why don't you hang around the house until we leave for town? Get some rest. Read a book."

"Call my family."

"Exactly. I've got some extra hands today, so everything's covered."

She lifted her coffee mug in a salute. "Perfect."

"Perfect," he said with a smirk. "See you at lunchtime."

As soon as the door closed behind him, she

slumped and dropped her head on the counter. A couple of more coffees and she'd call home to explain she was staying in Montana for Christmas.

The call to her parents went better than she'd expected. Her parents were disappointed. However, owning a ranch of their own, they understood that the work didn't stop just because people had a designated holiday on the calendar. In addition, they thought giving Russ the day off to be with his pregnant wife was just the kind of act that symbolized the Christmas spirit. Her mother made Wendy cry when she said Wendy's selflessness was one of the things that made her so special to everyone around her.

Her sister didn't take well to the news. At first, she tried to talk Wendy out of staying, using her son as a ploy. When that didn't work, Risa tried guilt. *Our parents are getting older. You'll miss so much of your nephew's first Christmas.*

And finally, her sister teared up, saying, "We've never been apart for Christmas."

"I know," Wendy had said. "But you have Trevor and your son now. You have your own family."

"But I still need you. You're like my left arm. You can't be my right arm because I'm right-handed, but still, my left is important too."

Wendy's eyes had tears even as she'd laughed. "Yeah. You're my left arm too. I'll be home before you know it."

Risa sniffed. "I know, and you're doing a good thing giving that couple a final Christmas together before the baby comes. I understand all that. I just want to be selfish and have you right across the hall so I know you're okay and safe."

"Love you," Wendy said.

"Love you, too."

After the family notifications were done, Wendy headed back to her room and set her alarm for noon.

When Zane came back to the house, it was close to one. Wendy had showered, dressed and was sitting in front of the fireplace with a romance novel she'd found.

"Feeling better?" he said before shoving his head in the refrigerator.

"Much. I needed that nap."

He pulled out a casserole dish of leftovers and put them in the microwave. Then he walked over to where she sat.

"Look, Wendy. You're a guest. You're not an employee. You don't have to get up early and take care of horses. You can sleep in as late as you want. Every day, if that's what you want."

She set the book in her lap. "I'm not doing a good job? You found something today that I've been doing wrong?"

"Oh, no." He sat on the arm of the matching chair. "Albert sneered at me today when I went in to clean his stall, but I've been thinking all day. I don't think I've been fair to you. You came here to rest and think. Instead, I've got you mucking stalls and exercising horses. I feel guilty that you haven't had the time to do what you want. Take today, for instance."

"What about today?"

"Instead of resting or reading a book, I'm dragging you off to decorate a community center for a Christmas Eve party."

She smiled. "Dragging me? Should I put my hair into a ponytail so you have something to hold as you drag me?"

He sighed. "You know what I mean. You don't have to go today. Really. I'm sure there'll be plenty of help."

"So you don't want me to go? Is that what you're saying?"

"No. Of course not. I'm giving you an out."

"And if I don't want an out? If I want to go?" She reached over and touched his knee. "Zane, I'm thirty-five years old. Nobody tells me what to do. Not before I came here, not now, and not in the future. If I didn't want to help with Sheila's project, I simply could have stayed at the ranch yesterday. No harm. No foul. But I didn't. I went into town and bought a crap-ton of toys to make some less fortunate kids have a better Christmas." She squeezed his knee. "It makes me happy to help. It makes *my* Christmas special. For me, Christmas has never been about what I get. My joy has always been in watching others open their gifts. That's what brings me happiness. And cowboy, you're not taking that away from me this year." She pulled her hand back into her lap.

"Yes, ma'am," he said just as the microwave timer beeped. "Let me grab some lunch and a shower, and then we'll head out. I have a couple of stops to make."

Wendy went back to her book while she waited.

However, the antics of the heroine could not pull her attention away from the sexy cowboy upstairs currently naked in the shower. Her mind drifted to wet skin, hot water pouring over her as she pressed herself against his firm chest, his rock-hard thighs, his granite-firm cock. She found her pulse rising and her breathing choppy as she imagined Zane's mouth working its way down from her aching breasts to her throbbing sex.

"You ready to go?"

Zane's question snapped her out of her daydream, and she leapt to her feet. "Ready, ready," she answered.

He grinned. "Were you asleep again?"

She guffawed. "No."

"Uh-huh," he said. "Let's go."

The drive to the community center of Gardiner took close to forty-five minutes in the snow that'd fallen since noon. But unlike the day she'd arrived, she wasn't clutching her hands or looking for the hand-holds. Zane had shown himself to be a good driver, and she felt safe in his hands.

In his hands. The phrase echoed in her head. She did feel safe with Zane. Oh, not her physical safety. She knew he'd never touch her if she didn't want him to. But emotionally.

Maybe Edie and Sheila were right about the woman in Chicago. Zane was dedicated to the ranch and the animals. Plus, he'd talked about his brother coming home and giving the dude-ranch business a serious try. No way would he have all these Montana plans if leaving were a genuine option for him.

He'd said he and Pricilla were friends before getting serious. Perhaps the phone call she'd overheard was just that…one friend consoling another friend. She'd been around Zane enough since she'd arrived to observe how he treated others, and it was always with respect and honesty. There is no way he would have kissed her like he did last night if he were involved with another woman. No way. That would be so far out of character from what she'd seen of him.

"You're quiet," he said.

"Just thinking."

"Good. That's what you're supposed to be doing, although I have to confess, I have no idea what you're supposed to be thinking about. All my mom told me was that you needed a place to think."

She chuckled. "Well, October and November were pretty bad months. December hadn't started off so great either. I needed some time to get away from my life and decide what I want to do with the rest of it."

"Rest of your life?"

"You got it."

"Sounds heavy." He sighed, looked at her, and then back to the road. "I haven't said anything about what happened to you, the whole jilted-bride thing, but I have to say that your groom was insane. He'd have to be totally out of his mind to walk away from you. You're an incredible woman. Beautiful. Sexy. Funny. Sweet."

Her head dropped to her chest. Yeah, she was

going to have to tell him everything, and she feared he would lose all respect for her if he believed she'd broken up her cousin's wedding. The truth was not all people believed she was an innocent party. There were those who saw her as a villainess who'd used and discarded a younger man, all while breaking her dear cousin's heart.

"Zane, I have something I need to tell you."

"You can tell me anything," he said.

When she hesitated, he added, "Anything, Wendy. There's nothing you can say that will change my opinion of you."

"I'll take that bet," she said and started into the non-wedding story.

He snorted in appropriate places, cussed when she told him how Roy had announced he was in love with someone else, and was visibly surprised when she confessed she had not been the bride at the fiasco, but had been the maid of honor the groom wanted to leave the bride to be with.

"Wow," he said. "Just, well, I don't know what to say. You never encouraged him?"

She rolled her eyes. Everyone asked that question, and she gave him the answer she gave everyone. "No. Never. All the time I spent with him was to help my cousin. Roy was quote unquote okay, but I'll be honest and say that my cousin is probably better off. If he could so misinterpret someone trying to help as someone coming on to him, I would place money on him not being a faithful husband."

"So your cousin…How is she doing?"

"Good. Went back to work and kept on moving. Mom mentioned that she thought Mae might be in Montana right now on a project but would be home for Christmas."

"Poor gal, but I think you may be right about the faithful-husband bit. When I lived in Chicago, I had a friend who believed every woman was coming on to him. Once in a restaurant, I couldn't convince him that the waitress was being nice to improve her tip rather than trying to flirt with him. Oh, no. He was sure she was wantin' him bad."

Both of them laughed.

"Bad thing was he was married to a wonderful woman. I never knew him to stray, but I didn't ask, either. I didn't want to know. If I ever hear of their divorce, I think I'll know exactly what happened. I hope not, but this guy's an idiot. A financial genus but a total buffoon when it came to social graces."

"Well, that's my story. I'm not a jilted bride. I'm just a hard-working doctor who got accused of something I didn't do. I simply wanted some time away to process."

"You know, you'll be screwed if the groom, what was his name? Roy? What if Roy decided to go away at Christmas to get his head together and everyone thinks the two of you have sneaked off?"

She glared at him. "You are not funny. God, that would be horrible. Maybe I need to check his whereabouts."

His loud laugh filled the car. He reached over and

patted her thigh. "Don't you worry. I can be your alibi."

"Argh," she said and banged her head on the back of the seat. "Don't even kid."

He was still chuckling when he pulled into the post office parking lot. "Be right back. Need to check the ranch box."

He came back with a stack of mail and a large box. He put it all in the back seat.

"Doing your Christmas shopping online?" she joked.

"Mom mailed something to me. I haven't done any Christmas shopping yet."

"Zane! Tomorrow is Christmas Eve. Have you lost your mind?"

"Kidding. I sent my brother his gift back in November. Ordered something for Mom and Dad and had it shipped directly to their place in Florida. I give Russ and Lori a cash bonus for Christmas. I'm all done. What about you?"

"I am the online shopping queen. Shopped, found, ordered and shipped everything last week. It didn't matter if I stayed here or went home. I knew my gifts were there."

They arrived at the community center a little after three. The Lancasters' van was pulled up to a loading dock, and a small army of helpers were taking out box after box of decorations and supplies.

"This looks like the place," he said and parked.

Zane was greeted like a warrior returning home from war. Wendy was welcomed with hugs and kind words. Everyone she met made her feel like she'd been a part of this community for years instead of weeks.

By seven, holly draped the walls. An eight-foot fir decked out in lights and ornaments dominated the small space. Wrapped toys and bicycles were placed behind the tree. Wendy had clapped and laughed when a large red Santa chair was brought in and placed near the tree. Then, a pair of doors closed, blocking the view of the gifts and the Santa chair. Only the tree was left visible in the room.

Six-foot tables ran around the outer rim of the room. Each table wore a red or green cloth with their edges trimmed in silver tinsel. Zane had told her these tables would be overflowing with food for the families to take home tomorrow at the end of the party.

The last decoration to go up was a sprig of mistletoe over the door.

"And we are done," Sheila announced, her hands cupping her mouth. "Thank you, everybody. You are each one a Santa that will make some child's Christmas one to remember. For my elves, please be here tomorrow by three. Families will begin arriving by four. My door protectors need to be in place by three-forty-five to keep the curious out of the present room. Any questions? Good. See you tomorrow."

Wendy followed the group to the stack of coats they'd shed upon entering. She was slipping her arms into hers when Sheila hugged her from behind.

"You're an angel," she whispered in Wendy's ear. "This year would have been hard for some of the kids. I mean, they'd have gotten something from Santa but you fulfilled a lot of wishes with your generous donation."

Wendy turned, her gaze sweeping the room to see if anyone was close enough to have overheard.

"No one heard me," Sheila said quietly. Then with much more volume, she blared out, "Thank you for helping with the decorations, Wendy. That extra pair of hands sure came in handy today." The older woman winked and walked away to thank others who'd come.

"How about we grab dinner while we're in town?" Zane said as he slipped on his coat.

"Sounds like a winner to me."

They were headed for the door when Cliff shouted, "Zane. Hold on a sec."

They stopped.

Cliff hurried over and pointed up. "Mistletoe. You have to kiss."

Zane grinned. "Gosh, is that what that means?"

He dipped Wendy and gave her a loud smack on the lips and stood her upright.

The room laughed and cheered.

When Zane released her, Wendy's head spun from the quick dip and back upright. She stumbled a little. She was tired of these kisses without follow through. Tonight, their flirtation would go further than a kiss on the steps if she had anything to say about it.

"Wow, man. That must have been some kiss," one of the guys called over. "She can barely stand."

Zane bowed and pointed to his mouth. "Kryptonite for women."

Wendy rolled her eyes. "Come on, Superman. Feed me." *And then take me home for dessert.*

It was close to ten-thirty when they finally pulled back into the ranch. There was a note tacked to the door from Russ asking that Zane come over no matter how late it was when he got home.

"Sounds serious." Wendy said. "You think something's wrong?"

He shrugged. "No clue. I'll head over and see what he needs."

"Want me to come? Maybe something's wrong with Lori and they need a doctor."

"Naw. If that were it, he would have asked you to come or called an ambulance. It's probably something with one of the owners."

He gave her a long, wet, deep kiss that had her head spinning again. He pressed his hard body against hers, trapping her between two solid objects…the wooden door and his deliciousness. She could feel his rigid cock digging into her abdomen.

When he broke the kiss and stepped back, he said, "Damn, Wendy. You make it hard to walk away, but I have to. First, because Russ left a note asking me to come by, and he never does that. And second…" He stepped to her and kissed her again. "Aw, hell. There is no second. Only something important could pull me away tonight."

She licked her lips, tasting him again.

"Don't do that," he demanded. "How the hell can I leave with you looking good enough to eat? Stop it."

"I'm not doing anything," she protested, but

inside, she was grinning her ass off. She knew exactly what she was doing. "I'll wait up for you…In my room."

He groaned. "I've got to go." He stepped away, then turned and walked down the steps. He turned back, shook his head, and she could hear him mutter, "This better be fucking important, Cowboy Russ."

She headed in and upstairs. The community center had required some cleaning before the decorations went up, and she'd dug in with the rest of the crew using brooms and mops. She felt like she had dirt and sweat over her entire body.

She started the shower running and stripped. For the first time, she didn't lock the door, using the rationalization that if Zane needed her—medically or otherwise—he'd be able to get in. And if she just happened to still be in the shower, and he wanted to join her—to save water, of course—then she wouldn't have to get out to unlock a door.

When the water cooled and then ran cold, an extremely disappointed doctor climbed out of the shower, dried off, and put on her sexiest, but warmest, pajamas and crawled between her sheets to wait.

Chapter Eleven

W hen Wendy woke, her room was dark, but she could see the moon through the slit in the curtains. Her fingers fumbled around on the bedside table until she found her phone and pulled it over to check the time. Three a.m. Hadn't Zane come home yet? With her blatant invitation, she was surprised—and disappointed--to wake alone.

Maybe he was still with Russ. That could mean only one thing. There was a problem.

She shook her phone, and the camera's flash came on, serving as a tiny flashlight. Using the small beam, she went to the bathroom, and then flushed. When everything was quiet again, she slowly opened the door that connected Zane's room to the small bath.

The room was pitch dark. She eased into the room and up to the bed…An empty bed. He hadn't come home.

Dressing quickly and warmly, she headed downstairs to go to the barn to see if she could be of assistance. The minute her foot hit the bottom step Pike's head popped up from the floor by the fireplace. The glow from the embers revealed a prone male body on the sofa, one arm thrown over his brow. Coda stood and walked over to her. She rubbed Coda's head and silently made her way back upstairs.

When she came down again at seven, Zane was gone, as were both dogs. She bypassed the coffee to head to the barn. She found Zane, Russ, and Lori in the east wing, an area she'd been in but never worked. All three were standing around the open door of stall five.

"Good morning," she said. "What's going on?"

Zane moved his gaze from the stall to her. "Good morning. What's going on is a pregnant mare."

"No kidding." She hurried forward to look in. "I didn't know you had a pregnant mare here."

The mare in question had the darkest black coat Wendy had ever seen. Her eyes looked toward Wendy. The mare was antsy, pacing and shaking her head.

"We don't or didn't until last night," Russ replied to Wendy's question. "Gus Henry found her on the road and brought her here, hoping she was one of ours. She isn't."

"Whose is she?"

Zane shrugged. "And that is the million-dollar question. No brand. No halter even. No identifier of any kind."

"I put her back here because it's the most isolated stall. If she's sick, I didn't want her around the other horses," Russ said. "Lori and I made calls last night, but no one's claimed her."

"So this was the note on the door?" Wendy asked.

"Yup. Russ was hoping I knew something about her, but I'm as clueless as he is."

"She is stunning," Wendy said, admiring the mare's shiny coat. "I can't remember ever seeing a black horse with blue eyes."

"Very rare," Zane said. "Happens, but not often, which is why I'm sure this gal belongs to someone who must be out of their mind with worry."

"Maybe you should call the vet," Wendy suggested. "If I were missing my prize horse, especially if she were pregnant, I'd make sure all the vets in the area kept an eye out for her."

"Way ahead of you," Zane said. "Called this morning. My vet is coming to check her out. None of the others had heard of a missing horse, or at least none of the ones I reached out to. It's Sunday and Christmas Eve. I'm sure there are families away on holiday. The owner might not even know she's missing yet."

"Bullshit," Wendy said. "An owner would have to be exceptionally irresponsible to leave a horse this far along in her pregnancy."

"I've known some fairly horrible owners," Russ said.

His wife nodded. "Remember the Owens family?"

"Don't remind me," Russ growled.

Lori looked at Wendy. "Terrible family. Beat and

misused their animals. Russ kicked the owner's ass and took their horses."

"That's stealing," Wendy observed. "Wasn't that a tad bit of a problem?"

"My dad paid the Owens for the horses but threatened to call the authorities if they got any more."

"What happened to them?"

"Moved to Las Vegas was the last thing I heard," Zane said.

"Good riddance," Russ said.

The mare snorted and shook her head as though agreeing with the sentiment.

"Well, she's a beauty and I hope she foals here. I want to see her baby."

"We're definitely keeping her here," Zane said. "I'll put out some alerts that we found a horse, but I didn't put much of a description except black, pregnant mare. I didn't mention her eye color and don't intent to. We need to keep that tidbit to ourselves. I wouldn't want someone to claim her who didn't own her. Got it?"

Russ saluted and Lori rolled her eyes at her husband's antics. She looked at Zane. "Good plan."

"Wendy," Zane said. "Would you mind working in this area and keeping other horse owners who come in today away?"

"Sure. I'll enjoy talking labor and delivery with her, not that I know the first thing about it personally. But from a medical standpoint, I've got tons of knowledge."

Lori laughed. "Maybe I need to pull up a chair and listen."

"Please do. We can have a ladies day in."

Russ brought Lori a chair while Zane hauled over a square bale of hay for Wendy.

"That's not right," Lori protested. "You should have brought her a chair, too."

"Trust me," Wendy said as she lowered herself to the bale. "I may have sat on as many hay bales as chair seats. Plus, if the cost of getting a chair is pregnancy, I'll just keep my bale, thank you very much."

About ten, the ranch vet, Dr. Peters, along with Zane and Russ strolled into the area.

"I hear I've got a patient," he said.

"And she's a beauty," Wendy replied, rising to her feet. She extended her hand to a man in his late forties or early fifties. "I'm Wendy McCool."

"I'm Dr. Peters, but call me Tim. Nice to meet you." After shaking her hand, he entered the stall. He approached the mare slowly, giving her time to adjust to his presence. "You're right, Zane. This has to be someone's prize horse, but she's not one of my patients. I would remember her." The vet ran his hand down the mare's nose, scratched her ears, and then palpated her abdomen. "Tell me, Zane, when were you last around a pregnant mare?"

Zane thought for a moment before replying, "Years, to tell you the truth. What about you, Russ?"

With a shake of his head, Russ said, "It's been a while. Since your dad stopped breeding horses a couple of years ago, we haven't had a pregnancy here since."

The vet looked over his shoulder at them. "So what's your guess for how far along she is?"

"She's ready," Zane said, and Russ nodded. "In fact, I hung around for a long time last night because I was concerned she would go into labor."

"Well, the good news is you're right. She is close. Not this moment, but I would say within the next twenty-four hours." Dr. Peters stepped out of the stall. "She appears healthy and well-cared for. I'll put out some feelers and see if I can locate her owner. I'm sure you've all noticed her unusual eye color."

They all nodded.

"But," Zane said. "We decided to keep that tidbit secret. I'm hoping it might help us separate the owner from those who might be trying to get a free horse."

The vet agreed. "Good idea. Well, she looks good for now. Call if you need me. For now, keep her confined and wait for the foaling. She'd probably rather be alone for the birth. Most horses do, but you do what you think you need to."

"Thanks, Tim," Zane said. "I'll walk you out."

"Okay, little momma," Wendy said in a cooing voice to the mare. "I've got stalls to muck and a gelding who's demanding my attention, so I've got to get to work." She shut the lower portion of the door.

"Yeah, me, too. I mean, not a gelding who needs my attention," Lori said with a laugh, "but some house cleaning to tackle."

. . .

ONCE THE VET PULLED FROM THE DRIVE, ZANE looked at Russ. "Don't forget you have tomorrow off."

The cowboy scoffed. "Like I could forget that."

"You and Lori going over to her folks' place for Christmas?"

"Yeah. We'd hoped to get away early afternoon. Should be back by late tomorrow. That still work?"

Zane nodded. "Sure does. Let's get busy and get done so we can all get an early night off."

At noon, Zane's phone rang. He set the pitchfork he was using aside and answered. "Zane Miller."

"This is Sheila Lancaster."

"Merry Christmas Eve, Sheila," he said. "Everything ready for tonight?"

"That's why I'm calling. I have a huge problem. I hope you can help."

Zane leaned on the stall wall and cocked his foot up on a bale of hay. "You know I will. What do you need?"

"Cliff threw his back out. He can barely walk. There is no way he can play Santa tonight. Tell me you'll do it for us this year."

The poor woman's voice shook with anxiety. He knew she must be stressed over her husband and today's party. The Christmas Eve event was so important to her.

"Of course, I'll do it. Do you want Wendy to come over and take a look at Cliff and see if she can help?"

"No!"

Her reply was so vehement and loud, Zane held the phone away from his ear. That was an odd response, especially since Sheila was one of the townspeople who'd been the most interested in having a doctor move to town. It seemed like to him that she'd take advantage of Wendy being here,

"No," she repeated a little more calmly. "He's done this before, and I'm sure he'll be fine in a day or so, but he can't sit in that chair holding kids in his lap or picking children up without doing more damage."

"Okay. No problem. Where's the Santa suit?"

"At the community center. Everything you'll need is there. The suit, the beard, the eyebrows, and even the fake stomach stuffing. I can't thank you enough for doing this."

"Wait. How will I know which present goes to which child?"

"There's a list. Easy peasy. Just follow the list. Thank you so much. Bye."

"Sheila?" He looked at his phone, but she was gone. A short telephone conversation with Sheila was a rarity, but the poor woman had obviously been rattled by her husband's injury.

But Sheila was always Santa's elf helper. Surely she'd be there to help him tonight. This was her baby. He had nothing to worry about, except finishing up on the ranch and getting down to the center in time to get into costume.

Luckily, an overabundance of owners showed up to work today, since no one wanted to come on Christmas day. But that extra help had him finished and headed to the house for a shower by one.

He'd already decided to get Wendy to go to the

community center with him to help, so he was a little surprised to see his mom's Jeep gone.

Inside the house, he found a note on the counter.

Gone to community center early. Sheila needed some extra help and asked me to come down. Borrowed the Jeep. Hope you don't mind. See you tonight.

Wendy

Last night, he'd had every intention of taking her to his bed. When she'd said she'd wait up, his cock had gotten so hard he feared it would break off in the cold as he'd walked to the barn.

When he'd finally gotten back, he'd gone straight to her room. She'd been asleep, her long hair spread across her pillow like it'd been arranged to look perfect. He thought about waking her. Even lifted his hand to touch her shoulder, but she looked so peaceful and happy. He couldn't bring himself to disturb her.

His lusty and dirty mind disagreed and protested loudly when he went back downstairs to drink a beer and chill. He'd settled on the couch and gotten a couple of hours of sleep before heading back out to check on their pregnant guest.

Tonight. Only he and Wendy would be at the ranch tonight with no one close enough to hear her scream his name as she came again and again. A smile twitched his mouth. Oh yeah, Santa had some plans for Wendy McCool and he hoped she would be a naughty, *naughty* girl tonight.

He pulled into the community center and parked

next to the Jeep. He was surprised to find only Wendy inside.

"Where is everyone?" he asked.

She shrugged. "I don't know. Sheila came by to let me in the building, drop off some boxes, and told me about Cliff's back. I offered to go over and examine Cliff, but she was adamant she didn't want me to." Gesturing to a box, she continued. "She told me you were taking Cliff's place and I was to be your helper. I guess she just assumed I would take hers. There's a notebook full of instructions. Maybe we should start there?"

"I suppose so."

"When was the last time you played Santa?"

He checked the time on his phone. "Oh, about two hours from now."

"Argh. I was hoping you could tell me what to do."

Seeing that they were alone, he moved in close and nuzzled his nose in her neck. "Baby, I'd love to tell you what to do."

She laughed and pushed him back. "Be serious."

He pumped his eyebrows. "I am serious." He sighed. "Fine, but we have some unsettled business for later tonight. For now, get the notebook, and let's see what's what."

They had an hour to review Sheila's instructions which were detailed down to the last song of the night.

"It's Playing Santa for Dummies," Wendy joked.

Zane pointed to his chest. "Perfect for this guy. Okay, let's get those costumes laid out and see what goes where."

The Santa outfit was exactly what he'd expected. Pants, coat, hat, strap-on black boots, fake beard, and fake eyebrows.

However, it was the helper elf costume that had his attention. Not having seen Sheila playing the role of helper elf in over a decade, he had a great deal of trouble envisioning Sheila ever wearing this.

First item from the box was a green hat trimmed in white faux fur, similar to his Santa hat except the color. Next were a pair of red and white striped stockings, followed by a short—as in micromini—red velvet dress trimmed with white fake fur like the hat. A short, green corset jacket made from a soft material like velvet was attached to the dress so it was all one piece. A piece of red satin with a green bow filled the space where the coat opened over the wearer's breasts. A black belt came next, followed by a pair of black heels.

Wendy held up the dress. "Are you kidding? This thing barely covers my ass. You cannot tell me that Sheila wore this."

Zane shrugged and bit back his grin. "I have no idea. I haven't been to one of these parties in years, but if that's what she left, I guess that's what you're supposed to wear."

God help his heart if she actually put that costume on. Santa with a permanent hard-on might be difficult to explain to the parents...Well, not the fathers, that's for sure.

"I don't know, Zane."

"Just try it on. Maybe the material is stretchy and hangs over the top of the stockings."

He hoped to hell it didn't.

"Fine, but if my ass is hanging out, then Santa has no helper this year, or has a helper wearing her jeans." She collected all the clothing in her arms and began walking.

"Where you going?"

"There has to be a ladies' room. I'll get dressed in there."

"Hang on. The men's room is right there, too. I'll see what I can do with mine."

It was almost three and other volunteers would be arriving soon. They both needed to get a move on with dressing.

The men's room was directly across from the ladies' room. After toeing off his boots, he stripped off his jeans and shirt, leaving on only his boxers, undershirt, and socks. The red velvet pants went on first, complete with suspenders to hold them up, which was helpful since they were huge. The padding was a little difficult to get strapped on as it fastened in the back. Grabbing the beard, eyebrows, and faux belly, he crossed over to the ladies' room for Wendy's help.

"Hey," he said as he entered. "I need—Holy shit, Wendy."

His eyes must have bugged out of his head. He locked the door behind him and studied his helper elf. He'd had some fairly erotic daydreams about what he wanted to do with and to his guest. But he'd never envisioned her like this. He was old enough to appreciate the fact that sometimes a woman in a racy outfit could be a hundred-times sexier than a naked woman. Today was one of those days.

Lord alive. What a vision. He went rock hard in seconds.

The stockings started about four inches above her knees and ended in a pair of black, high heel shoes. The flared skirt hit a few inches below her ass, leaving at least three to four inches of exposed thigh. Her breasts were smashed into the small top, leaving mounds of luscious flesh overflowing the material. She was fastening the black belt around her waist when he entered.

Their gazes caught in the mirror.

"I don't know about this, Zane. I feel a little exposed."

"Damn. You look good enough to eat."

He stalked across the room, feeling every bit like a predator after prey.

"I'm going to have a hard-on all night."

She twisted her hips side to side. "Oh, yeah?" She frowned. "You think I look good in this then?"

He advanced on her, and she backed up until a wall sink stopped her.

"Have I ever told you I have a serious fetish about elves?"

She laughed. "You are such a perv."

He dropped to his knees, and she gasped.

"What are you doing?"

"Your legs look like candy canes, and I'm craving some of your sweetness."

"Zane," she protested, but it was weak.

"I can smell you." His nose pressed into the crease between her thighs. "You smell like a fantasy come to life."

He slid his hands up the insides of her legs, up her calves to her thighs. If she protested, he'd stop, but he prayed to every power under the sun that she wouldn't say stop.

She didn't.

When his hands were between her thighs, he pushed gently. "Open for me, baby."

The pointed heels tapped on the tile floor as she stepped her feet apart. She grabbed the rim of the sink as though it was the only thing keeping her upright. What he wanted was to see her melt to a point where nothing would support her legs.

He moved his hands farther up until he came to her panties. The crotch was soaking wet. He took a deep inhale and then blew a warm stream of air across that dampness. She shivered in response.

"You're wet," he said. "So fucking wet. You like this, like the thought of this. I'm going to put my tongue so far up inside you, I'll have your taste in my mouth instead of my own."

He caught her panties in his mouth and sucked. She moaned, and the fingers of her hand threaded through his hair and pulled. The pain was erotic and drove him crazy with need. He tongued her through her panties, shoving the material up and inside her canal.

Her hips bucked and she spread her feet wider to give him better access. Slipping a finger into the elastic of her bikini panties, he worked them down her legs, forcing her to close her stance so he could remove them.

"Santa likes elves who do what he wants," he growled and then ran his tongue up the slit of her sex. Her musk and sexual arousal coated his tongue and made his cock as hard as granite. Using his fingers, he separated her folds, licked her from front to back before thrusting his tongue deep inside her.

"God," she moaned as she ground against his mouth. "Make me come, Zane. I need you to…"

He replaced his tongue with his middle finger, shoving it deep. He added a second finger as his tongue found her clit. He circled the hard nub as his fingers pumped in and out of her.

She matched his rhythm, timing the movement of her hips with his fingers.

On either side of his head, her thighs began to quake, and he knew she was close. He pressed the flat of his tongue against her nub and she cried out as her muscles tightened and shook with her release.

When her climax ended, she sighed and slumped against the sink.

"Wow, Santa. You know some cool tricks."

He stood and chuckled. "You've been a dirty, dirty elf, Wendy McCool. Doing this in a public bathroom. Santa may have to punish you went we get home."

"Oh, really? And here I was thinking I was going to owe Santa a favor or two or three later."

A banging on the locked door interrupted them.

"Santa? You in there? It's time to get started. I'll leave your coat on the door knob."

"That sounded suspiciously like Sheila Lancaster," Wendy said.

"Didn't it though? Help me with this stupid belly and beard."

"I'll do that, and then I'm getting out of this outfit."

Zane looked at her and grinned. "I can help with that."

"You've done enough. Maybe later I'll let you unhook my bra."

He snapped his fingers. "I'm a pro."

"Hmm. I'm not sure if that's good or bad."

She kissed him and tasted herself.

"Wash your face and get me off you," she said with a laugh.

By the time he was buttoning up the velvet coat, he was almost back to normal, if craving the taste of Wendy again was his new normal. Might be, and funny enough, he was okay with that.

He took his place in the big red chair and waited for the doors to open, a little nervous that he would somehow mess things up. Wendy came out of the ladies' room dressed back in her jeans and Christmas-themed shirt. She had the elf hat on her head however.

"Think we should take the elf costume home for later?" she said. "You seem to appreciate the work-manship of the construction."

He laughed.

"That's ho-ho-ho, Santa," Sheila Lancaster said as she slipped through the door. She frowned at Wendy. "Where's your elf costume?"

"I'll tell you what, Sheila. If you can produce even one picture or one eyewitness who can confirm you've worn that in previous years, then I'm game. I'll go put it on. However..."

Sheila grinned and swept her hand from her green hat, past her red shirt, and down to her flannel pants. "My elf costume."

"You're a bad, bad woman," Wendy said, narrowing her eyes at the older woman.

"I think you rock, Sheila," Zane said with a laugh. "Um, can Wendy borrow the elf clothes for later?"

Sheila pointed her finger at both of them, laughed, and said, "Here we go. Grab the list, Wendy, and call off names. I'll locate the gift and pass it to Santa."

The doors to the hall opened, and the night started.

The stream of children seemed never ending. Zane ho-ho-hoed until his chest hurt. Some of the younger kids cried when they were put into his lap, but that didn't stop the parents from pictures. Even though he felt like he'd been sitting on the big red chair all night, it only took a couple of hours to go through the gifts.

Dinner was put on the tables around the room. Families dished up meals while trying to convince their children to stop riding bikes or shooting nerf balls at each other long enough to eat.

Zane stood and stretched his back. His spine popped a couple of times as he rotated his shoulders from side to side.

"Good job," Cliff Lancaster said as he walked up biting meat off a turkey leg.

"Wait a minute. I thought you were hurt."

"Yeah, me, too. Turns out I wasn't. Good thing, right?" He slapped Zane on the back and walked off.

Zane smelled a rat. He suspected those two were up to something and after seeing that elf costume, he figured they were trying their hand at matchmaking between him and Wendy. The old buzzards.

He walked around the room, giving each child a hug before he got out of costume and character. As he was nearing the stage ready to make his exit, the entry door flung open and his worst nightmare walked in.

"Santa, baby. I'm here for Christmas."

Chapter Twelve

Wendy stood next to Edie drinking ice water. "And then you wouldn't believe the elf costume she had for me to wear."

"Um, I might. Striped hose, mini dress, green hat?" Edie asked.

"Exactly. How did you know?"

"Good guess?"

Wendy propped her left hand on her waist. "No, not good guess."

Edie giggled. "It's mine. Frank bought it for me a few years ago. We might have played Santa and the bad elf a few times."

"You're kidding." She studied Edie. "You're not kidding."

"It's been cleaned, but I never expected you to actually wear it. It was, you know, supposed to, um, encourage Zane."

Wendy laughed. "Encourage? You're lucky that thing is coming home in one piece."

"Oh, you bad elf," Edie said, slapping Wendy's arm. "Tell me more."

Before Wendy could, the door to the community center opened and a tall, shapely woman entered. She looked out of place among this group. She wore black leggings with a pair of pencil-point heeled boots that came to her knees. Her long, sleek, dark hair shone under the ceiling's florescent bulbs like she'd weaved twinkling lights between the stands. Her thick coat was made of black mink, if Wendy's eyes didn't deceive her. Her face was gorgeous, like should-be-on-a-billboard gorgeous. Her cheeks were pink from the cold while her lips were puffy and red, as if she'd recently been making out with someone.

Beside her, Edie gasped and muttered, "Oh, fuck a duck."

The woman extended her arms and called, "Santa, baby. I'm here for Christmas."

"Um, Edie, who is that? Tell me that's not Priscilla."

Edie didn't say anything.

Wendy watched as Santa Zane crossed the room in four long strides. The woman threw her arms around his neck and tried to kiss him. He unwrapped her arms and pulled her toward the restroom area. As soon as they disappeared from sight, Edie groaned.

"You didn't answer my question. Who is that?"

"You know who it is. That bitch from Chicago. I

can't believe she had the nerve to come here and crash this party."

Wendy's heart dropped to her knees. She fought against the tears building in her eyes.

"I need to go," she said to Edie and sat her water bottle on the table behind them.

"Wait," Edie said. "I'm sure there's an explanation."

"Don't want to hear it."

She patted the pockets in her jeans and found her keys. "Merry Christmas, Edie." Pulling her keys from her pocket, she headed for the door.

"Your coat," Edie yelled.

Wendy didn't care if she had her coat or not. Edie's shout didn't even slow her march across the room. She would not cause another public scene over a guy.

She threw open the door and walked into a thirty-mile-an-hour wind and temperatures in the upper twenties. Who cared if she froze to death? Well, her parents and sister would care, but Zane was probably in the ladies' room playing Bad Santa with Priscilla.

The Jeep groaned but started. She pulled out of the parking lot and toward the ranch. She checked motel signs as she drove through town. Vacancies everywhere. She'd have no trouble finding a room tonight.

She'd driven fifteen miles before the first blast of heat hit her legs. She was so cold the heat on her flesh should hurt, but she was pretty numb.

How could she be so stupid? Zane had never said

he was over Priscilla. Edie and Sheila had told her that, and she'd elected to believe them. How could a well-educated thirty-five-year-old woman make such bad decisions?

As she turned on the ranch road, the vet's white SUV was idling ready to pull out. She stopped and rolled down the window.

"Everything okay?" she asked.

"Russ called me. Didn't want to bother Zane. Your mare foaled about an hour ago. Stunning black colt."

Her heart sighed. She did love baby horses. "And the colt? He's doing good?"

"Perfect. Mom did a great job with delivery and is nursing her boy. I know you're going to sneak in there and see them, but be quiet. Mom is a little skittish."

"Tell me you found the owner."

"Nope. Got feelers out, but no one is stepping up to claim her."

"That's crazy."

"Agreed. Tell Zane to give me a call day after tomorrow unless there is a problem."

"Will do."

She'd write him a note and leave it. She wasn't planning on speaking to him again…at least not in this life time.

However, there was no way she was leaving without seeing the new baby. Instead of parking near the house, she drove down to the barn and parked. The wind howled as she exited the car. Wrapping her arms around herself, she hurried to the small door on the side of the barn and let herself in. Horses nickered at her. The aroma of fresh straw and horse oats filled her nose. She was going to miss this.

Turning on the light on her phone, she made her way to the east wing and down to stall five. Two people stood a few steps away from the closed bottom of the Dutch door.

"Hey," she whispered. "I thought you two would be gone by now."

Russ quirked up the side of his mouth. "If you think I can drag my wife away from a new colt, you have another think coming."

"I couldn't leave," Lori whispered. "She was in labor when we were scheduled to go, and there was simply no way I was going to leave her here on her own. What are you doing here? Shouldn't you be at the party?"

"Party was still swinging when I left, but I was tired," Wendy said. "I ran into Dr. Peters when I turned in. He told me about the baby. I'm dying to look."

"There's a warming light in there," Russ said. "You can look over the door."

"Good momma?" Wendy asked Russ as she walked past.

"The best."

Wendy looked over the door and smiled. Mom was standing and eating. The shiny, all-black colt with wobbly legs stood beneath her, nursing with gusto. She turned back to the couple and clutched her chest. "My heart exploded."

Lori chuckled. "And now you know why I couldn't

leave. Seriously, I can see my family anytime, but a new colt? Now that's special."

"And on Christmas Eve, too. That's what we should call the mom. Eve."

"I like it, but don't get attached," Russ warned. "Somebody will claim her."

"And if they do, I'll buy her and the baby," Wendy said with determination.

"What's with all the whispering?"

Wendy's back stiffened as Zane walked up.

"Had the baby while you were gone," Russ said. "How did you know to come down?"

"Saw the Jeep parked down here. Why aren't you two gone?"

Russ tilted his head toward his wife. "Her decision to stay."

"What are you doing here?" Wendy asked. "Shouldn't you be with Priscilla?"

"I didn't know she was coming," Zane answered.

"That's our cue to leave," Russ said and grabbed his wife's arm. "Since I'm here, I'll be up and out in the morning, boss, so take all the time you need tomorrow. Come on, honey."

Lori blew a kiss toward the stall. "Bye, Eve. Bye, baby."

"Eve?" Zane said.

"Doesn't matter," Wendy said. "I'll get packed and be out of your hair in twenty minutes."

She whirled to leave, but Zane caught her wrist and pulled her to him. She struggled against his hold.

"Let me go," she demanded.

"Not until you listen to me."

"There's nothing you have to say that I want to hear."

"I didn't know she was coming," he ground out through clenched teeth. "I was as surprised as you were when she walked in."

"Don't you get it? I don't care. I refuse to be your side piece."

She pulled at her arm but he tightened his grasp.

"You're not my side piece. I'd rather you be my main piece. Don't leave. Stay."

"Oh, that'll be fun. Me, you, and your fiancée."

"We're not engaged. We're over. I've told her that."

"Maybe you did and maybe you didn't. All I know is that if she's in your house and going to be staying there, I will not sleep under the same roof."

"I understand, Wendy. I do. Don't leave. I want you to stay. Let her stay tonight and I promise she'll be on a plane out of here tomorrow, even if I have to buy a damn plane."

He pulled her against him and wrapped her in his arms. "You're like an icicle." He briskly rubbed her arms. "Where's your coat?"

"I don't know. I just left when I saw you walk away with her."

"I wasn't walking away with her. I was dragging her out of the room. It'd be just like her to call me Zane in front of the kids."

Her head dropped to his shoulder. "She's so beautiful."

"She is," he agreed. "Very beautiful but it's only skin deep. She has no substance. She isn't you." Hugging her tight, he said, "Come back with me. I'll put her in my parents' room for tonight, and tomorrow, she's gone."

"Does she know that she's leaving tomorrow?"

"Yes, I've told her that. Just like I've told her a million times that I'm not going back to Chicago and we are done." He leaned back until he could look into her eyes. "Trust me. Please."

"There are a ton of hotel vacancies in town. Why don't you take her to one of those hotels?"

He rested his forehead on hers. "I'm not in love with her, but she's a friend. She's here because her parents went to Aruba for Christmas and she's lonely. She doesn't have many friends."

Wendy arched an eyebrow. "I wonder why."

He kissed her. "She's only an old friend from my previous life. That's it. Nothing more. Trust me."

She inhaled and blew out a long breath. "I'll try."

"That's all I ask."

When they got to the house and entered, both border collies were sitting at the door. In the living room, Priscilla, still wrapped in her fur, sat on the edge of a sofa cushion.

"You're back," she said. "Can you turn on some heat? I'm freezing. Is this your renter?" She stood and extended her hand. "I'm Priscilla Roth." She glanced at Zane and then continued, "Zane's fiancée. I mean ex-fiancée," she said with a giggle.

"I'm Wendy McCool." She didn't take the

extended hand. Instead, she held them up like this was a robbery. "Sorry. I've touched the hands of a bunch of kids. I wouldn't want to spread germs."

Mostly, it was Priscilla's germs she didn't want.

Wendy came from money—lots and lots of money. There was very little she couldn't have had growing up. Instead of pampering their daughters, her parents had made her and Risa do the work their ranch hands did. She'd herded cattle, branded, mucked—you name a nasty job, and she'd done it. She and Risa were responsible for cleaning their own bedrooms and once a week, they teamed up to cook the family dinner.

Looking at the pretentious woman standing in front of her reeking of privilege and entitlement, Wendy made a note to call her parents and tell them thank you for making her work her ass off. But for her parents and their philosophy about work and responsibility, this could have been her. She shivered at the realization.

"Oh, I understand completely," Priscilla said, lowering her arm. "Kids can be nasty, can't they? And those parents?" She gave a dramatic cringe. "I mean, I know we have people living in the U.S. who don't have much, but the least they could have done is get new outfits for tonight. Know what I mean?"

Wendy smiled. "Oh, I understand you completely." She turned to Zane. "I'll say good night now. I'm sure you and your guest have some catching up to do. Good night."

She started up the stairs but Zane caught her arm. "Want me to walk you up?"

"Zane," Priscilla said. "I'm sure by now the woman knows how to get to her room."

Wendy looked at Priscilla. "And once again, I understand exactly what you mean. Good night."

Before she could break free from his hold, Zane pulled her close and kissed her. It wasn't a long kiss. Not like the ones they'd been sharing, but it was long enough to send Priscilla a message.

When he finally released her, he said, "Good night. See you in the morning."

She went to her room, her lips still tingling. Once there, even with the door shut, she could hear muffled voices until late into the night. The voices didn't keep her awake. During med school and residency, she'd trained herself to ignore lights and voices, but tonight, sleep was evasive. She tried every trick she knew, but her eyelids were glued open, and her ears tuned to every sound.

Finally, at close to one, she heard Zane speaking quietly to Priscilla. Their voices faded as they moved away, toward his parents' room was her guess. A few minutes later, the click of Zane's door echoed in her room like a gunshot. The shower between their rooms came on and went off a short time later.

At some point, she must have fallen asleep, because the next thing she was aware of was sunbeams reflecting off her floor. She checked the time, surprised to see she'd slept until after eight. She dressed and headed to the kitchen with her fingers crossed Zane had found a flight for Priscilla.

Her second surprise of the day, besides having

slept so late, was finding Zane in the kitchen, his brows pulled down in a frown. His expression was not one of happiness.

"Tell me you found her a ticket back to Chicago."

"Oh, I found her a ticket. Cost me an arm and a leg, but I got it."

She walked over and put her hand on his arm. "You look upset. What's wrong? Don't tell me it's the colt."

The squeeze he gave her hand didn't reassure her. "Priscilla's sick."

"Bull. She's playing you."

"No, she's sick. I went in to wake her and get her to the airport, and all she could do was groan. She's burning up with fever. Shakes and chills. Even a cough. She's really sick. I feel bad for her."

She gave a derisive snort. "Not buying it. I'll go see her. She can't fool me."

"I'll go with you."

Upstairs, Wendy flung open the door and marched into Zane's parents' room. What greeted her was not what she had expected.

The woman in the bed looked at her with glassy eyes. There were multiple layers of covers over her, all topped with her mink coat. Even still, she was shivering and coughing.

"Priscilla, did you have a flu shot this year?"

She shook her head. "Meant to, but I never found the time. I feel horrible. I ache all over."

Wendy looked at Zane. "Do your parents' have a thermometer?"

He shrugged. "I have no idea. I can look around in their bathroom."

"No," she said. "It's better if you aren't in here. I'm pretty sure she has the flu. She can't travel like this. She'd expose every person she comes in contact with." She looked at Priscilla. "Did you have any symptoms before you got here?"

"Not really," she replied with a cough. "Didn't feel good, but I've been busy, you know? I had to go to at least ten different Christmas parties this month. I thought I was just worn out."

Poor gal. Ten Christmas parties. Working so hard. Wendy wanted to roll her eyes and make some snide remark. Only her professionalism held her back.

"Stay in bed. I'll see what flu meds I can get my hands on. You can't leave this room today and maybe tomorrow."

Priscilla pulled the covers up to her nose. "Zane said you're a doctor. You need to do something."

Wendy ground her back molars together.

"Now, Priscilla," Zane said in a soothing tone. "Dr. McCool will do all she can. You need to thank her instead of being a brat."

"I'm not a brat," the insufferable woman said. "I'm sick. She's a doctor. It's her job to make me feel better."

"Stay in bed," Wendy said again and shut the door. She and Zane stood in the hall. "Tell me you had a flu shot this year."

His face flushed. He grimaced. "I meant to, but

you know how busy the ranch gets." He shrugged. "Forgot."

She growled deep in her throat. "At least tell me your only exposure to Ms. Prissy Flu was being in the same room. Tell me you didn't touch her."

This time, his gaze dropped to the floor, and he muttered a harsh cussword.

"What am I dealing with, bucko?"

He flinched. "She kissed me."

Wendy's life was a roller coaster. Up. Down. Swing around a sharp curve and drop again. She wanted to blame Roy for getting her on this damnable ride, but even she wasn't that naïve.

"Thank goodness, I had the sense to get a flu shot."

"So you won't get sick?" Zane asked with a hopeful expression.

"Still could. Since she didn't have much in the way of symptoms last night, I'm hoping we've caught it early. There is a new flu med that came out recently. Only one dose as opposed to a five-day treatment, but it's a little pricey."

"Trust me. I don't want Priscilla here for five days. It doesn't matter what it costs, if you can find it, buy it."

"Okay, but with today being Christmas, getting some in my hands will be a challenge. I know the small pharmacy here will be closed. What's the closest big city?"

"Bozeman. It's about an hour from here."

"I'll get online and see what might be open there.

In the meantime, you stay away from Russ and Lori, especially Lori. In fact, stay away from everybody, but horses. If you start running a fever or start feeling bad, let me know immediately."

As luck would have it, there was a large chain pharmacy open in Bozeman on Christmas day. Their hours were shortened because of the holiday, but she had time to get there before they closed. She was thinking about prescription forms and not having a Montana medical license when she remembered what she'd done for one of her patients who'd been on vacation in Florida.

Wendy didn't hold a medical license in Florida, only Texas. However, she'd called in the antibiotic her patient needed to a pharmacy in Dallas that belonged to the same chain and they transferred the prescription to where the patient was in Florida. That should work for her today.

By the time she'd driven to Bozeman and found the pharmacy, her local Dallas pharmacy had taken her verbal order for Xofluza and transferred the prescriptions to Montana. To be on the safe side, she'd ordered doses for Priscilla and Zane. Given the exchange of mouth germs, she'd be shocked if he didn't get the flu.

Yeah, she didn't get shocked. By that evening, Zane admitted he didn't feel right, but he blamed the late night and having to do a lot of the work today.

Wendy had Zane change Priscilla's ticket for Chicago to December twenty-seventh. No easy feat, but he got it done.

Wendy took all the moaning and grousing she could from the spoiled, entitled princess. Priscilla had complained her soup wasn't hot enough and the orange juice wasn't cold enough. She'd whined that Wendy wouldn't let Zane come into the room and visit. She was bored. There was nothing on television. She couldn't understand why Wendy hadn't picked up Vanity Fair and Cosmopolitan for her since she'd been at the drugstore any way.

When Wendy finally collapsed in her bed, she decided if Priscilla couldn't fly out soon, she might strangle her and sign the death certificate herself.

At first, her dreams were about her medical residency days, demanding patients, and surgeries gone bad. Finally, she settled into a nice dream where she was riding a horse on a beautiful spring day, the wind in her hair, flowers sprinkled among the fresh green grass.

A sound jarred her awake. She listened. She heard the moan first, followed by a groan.

She got out of bed, threw on her robe, and followed the sound to Zane's room. He was tossing and turning, wrapping himself in the covers. A low moan like the one that had awakened her rolled from his bed.

"Zane?" she whispered as she made her way to his side. "Zane? You okay?"

"Sick," he groaned out.

She popped on her phone light until she located a lamp beside the bed. As she flicked it on, Zane covered his eyes with his forearm.

"I'm dying," he announced solemnly. "Tell my parents I love them and will see them on the other side."

She couldn't stifle the snicker. Man flu. Was there any worse disease?

"Serves you right for letting Priscilla kiss you."

"I didn't let her," he protested.

"Whatever. I'll go get that dose of flu med I picked up."

"I'll need something to eat."

"No, it's okay. You can take this on an empty stomach."

He groaned. "No. I can't swallow a pill with water. I have to eat something."

She rolled her eyes. "Seriously? Fine. What do you need?"

"Cookie. Cracker. Anything that I can chew up and put the pill in to swallow."

She came back with three crackers, some orange juice and the pill. As he'd said, he used the crackers to take the med and then drank the juice.

"When will I get well?" he said with a pitiful tone.

"In time to drive Priscilla to the airport, I hope," she said. "Because if I have to drive that...that..."

"I know," he said. "Thank you.

He rolled over and fell asleep.

Back in her room, she knew her night was done and didn't even try to go back to sleep. As it was close to five a.m., she dressed, and headed to the kitchen resigned to her fate of caring for two flu patients.

Chapter Thirteen

If the next forty-eight hours were indicative of the rest of Wendy's life, she would give in and crawl in a hole to die. She'd always joked about man flu, but man flu combined with bitchy, entitle brat flu was more than any sane woman should be forced to endure.

Lori was ordered to stay away from the ranch house until such time the flu patients were better. That meant Wendy not only did all the cooking and cleaning, marginal that it was, but she went up and down stairs all day. Zane stayed in his bed, as ordered. Since he felt like death warmed over—his words—he didn't try to argue.

The flu medication did wonders for Priscilla. At least enough that she could get out of bed the day after Christmas. Regrettably, the woman claimed to not feel well enough to fix her own meals or get her own drinks. She perched herself on the sofa and waited for Wendy to fulfil her needs.

Wendy prayed hourly for Zane to recover so she didn't have to drive Priscilla to the Bozeman airport to put her on the plane back to Chicago.

Late on the evening of the twenty-sixth, there was a knock at the ranch door. She opened it to find Cliff and Sheila Lancaster on the front porch, each of them holding large boxes.

"Hey. You can't come in," Wendy said immediately.

"Don't plan to," Sheila said. "Edie called me about what's happening here. You poor girl. I got the ladies to put together some casseroles so you didn't have to make dinners. Just pop these in the oven, and they'll be good to go."

Wendy sighed. "I would kiss you, but that's probably not a good idea."

Sheila laughed. "Thank you but no. Edie would have come, but I didn't think it would be a good idea with her being pregnant."

"You made the right call. Did you two get flu shots this year?"

"Are you kidding?" Cliff said. "Do you realize how many people come into our store with runny noses and coughs? Of course we did. That's why we elected ourselves to bring over the dishes, but we're smart enough to go no farther."

"If you'll set the boxes right inside the enclosed porch, it'll keep the dogs out of them."

The Lancasters slid the boxes out of their arms and onto the porch.

"Thank you. I mean it," Wendy said. "This is a lifesaver."

"When is *she* leaving?" Sheila asked with a nod toward the house.

"Fingers crossed for tomorrow. We keep changing her ticket because she doesn't feel well enough to travel. I hope Zane will feel well enough to drive her to Bozeman to catch her flight. I'll do it if I have to, but an hour in the car with that woman might be the straw that breaks this camel's back. I guess I could gag her the whole way."

"Edie said to tell you that Frank will take her. Call Edie when we leave."

"Bless him. I'll call her."

"Need any help with the horses?" Cliff asked.

"Nope. Word got around that Zane was sick and we've had so much help, that most of the work is finished by noon."

"Now, you take care of yourself, too" Sheila said. "I'd hug you but…"

Wendy held up her hands. "That's close enough. Hug, hug."

Early on the morning of the twenty-eighth, Frank Dale—bless his heart—picked up Priscilla to take her to the airport. Zane insisted on riding along, and that was fine with Wendy. A quiet, empty house was like cold aloe on a burn. Blissful.

A large contingent of owners showed up that morning to take horses out for rides. She guessed that with the cold but sunny day, most people were anxious to get out.

It'd been days since she'd gotten to see the colt, so once the house was empty, she dressed in warm layers and headed down for a peek. She should have been surprised to find Lori there since the woman spent almost no time in the barns, but she wasn't. All of Lori's maternal hormones were probably in overdrive.

"How's everybody?" Wendy asked.

"Beautiful. Gorgeous. Incredible." Lori sighed. "Isn't birth amazing?"

Wendy smiled. "It sure is," she replied, not at all sure she would ever join that club. "Have they been out?"

"Oh, yes. Russ has had Eve and the baby out. He needs a name. We can't keep calling him baby or the colt."

"Dangerous thing to name an animal."

"Hey, you started it with Eve."

Wendy chuckled. "Guilty as charged. I can't believe we haven't heard a thing about the owner or a missing horse."

Lori shrugged. "The holidays maybe?"

"Maybe, but still, that is one of the most beautiful horses I've ever seen. Someone has to be looking for her,"

"Dr. Peters came out the day after Christmas. He drew some blood on Eve and everything is as it should be. No health issues."

"That's good to hear."

"He's as baffled as we are about where she came from."

"Well, I'm sure Zane will let her stay here until the owner is found. And if the owner is never found, I'll see if Zane will let me buy her and her baby and take them home with me to Texas."

"So you are going home?"

"Yeah."

"When? I thought Russ told me you would be here for a couple of months."

"I'll probably go home after the first of the year. I need to get back to my real life."

Lori sighed. "I was getting used to having you around. Gets lonely being the only woman on the place. I'd thought that maybe you and Zane…?"

"Nope. By the way, the Lancasters and Dales filled the food pantry at the house. There are tons of casseroles in the freezer. I meant to call you yesterday and tell you to come help yourself, but the day got away from me."

"I saw Frank Dale's truck early this morning. Tell me the phantom flu menace is gone."

"She's gone."

"Great. In that case, I'll come raid the freezer."

Before the men got back from Bozeman, Wendy called Edie to thank her again for the food.

"It was the least I could do," Edie said. "I was afraid to come to the house."

"Oh, I know. The flu bug is bad this year."

"I wasn't worried about catching the flu. I was

worried I might catch the bitch bug from
that woman."

Wendy chuckled. "I don't see that ever happening
to you."

"Thank you."

"Listen, I wanted to let you know that I'll be going
home after the first of the year."

"No! You can't. We're just getting to be good
friends."

"I came here to think and I've had plenty of time
to do that. I've made some decisions that I need to
implement in my life back in Texas. I'll miss you and
I'll hate not being here when your baby comes. You'll
have to send pictures and texts. Promise me you will."

"Well, this just sucks. What if Zane asked you to
stay? It's obvious to everyone that he's crazy for you
and I know you've got feelings for him. Shouldn't you
stay here and see what develops?"

Edie's words stung just like the tears building in
her eyes. Yeah, she'd love to stay, love to explore these
feelings she had, but...She sighed.

"He hasn't asked me to stay. In fact, he's given no
indication that he wants me to be here after the first of
the year."

"Cut him some slack. He's been sick."

"I have. He's had every opportunity to make his
feelings known, but I can't tread water waiting. I have
to go home at some point and this seems like the
right time."

"Well then, we have to say our goodbyes with a
loud, raucous party where the neighbors would call

the cops if they weren't partying along with the rest of us. Frank and I have been discussing having a New Year's Eve party this year since next year, I'll be too exhausted with two kids, four dogs, and one husband to wrangle. Let's do it. Party at our house. We'll ring in the new year right."

"Sounds great. Champagne for me. Sparkling grape juice for you."

Edie laughed. "I'll round up the usual crowd for the night. Let's say be here about seven."

"Let's potluck it so you don't have to do everything."

"Sure. Potluck and BYOB."

AS MUCH AS WENDY WANTED TO PRETEND ZANE'S ex-fiancée hadn't barged into the cozy world she had with Zane, Priscilla had. And with that interruption, the dynamics between them changed. Sure, she and Zane continued to work together, flirt, and sneak kisses from time to time, but she wasn't sensing the drive for the bedroom from Zane that he'd so clearly demonstrated on Christmas Eve.

And they talked for hours. However, none of their conversations were about Priscilla or what had happened over Christmas. Wendy didn't bring up leaving or the possibility of a future for them. Best she could tell, he'd had second thoughts about pursuing anything beyond the kisses—as nice as those were.

She was attracted to him—*really* attracted to him. What she felt for him was maybe more than she'd ever felt for any man. When they were in the same room, her heart raced. The palms of her hands sweated when he smiled at her. Her breath hitched when he hugged her. In bed, she swaddled herself in blankets and tried to sleep.

If she didn't know better, she'd think her symptoms were due to the flu. Except she did know better. It wasn't the flu. It was much worse…An unrequited love.

On December 30, the day started out as usual. Coffee, breakfast, chit-chat, then down to the barn to see to the horses. Wendy had fallen completely under the spell of the colt, Nicholas.

Against warnings from Zane and Russ, she and Lori had named him. The guys cautioned them they were getting too attached to the mare and her colt, and their hearts would be broken when the owner stepped forward.

The ladies ignored them.

Wendy found Eve and Nicholas in the corral. She climbed to the top rail and sat to watch, like she had every day. The colt kicked up his heels and ran circles around the arena and his mother. Like mothers everywhere, Eve tolerated her son's antics with a calm patience.

"I'm going to miss those two," Zane said joining her at the corral fence. He climbed up and sat beside her on the rail.

Wendy startled at his words. "What? You found the owner?"

"Yes and no. The owner was a horse breeder

who was shot and killed during a burglary on Christmas Eve. Our Eve was one of five horses stolen."

"Oh my God. That's horrible."

"I agree. The breeder lived here in Montana. Her family lives out East. The murder and theft were not discovered until her family arrived the day after Christmas."

"That poor family. This just gets worse and worse. How did you find out? Can we buy Eve and Nicholas? Are they for sale?"

He put his hand on her knee and Wendy's heart shattered.

"It was one of Dr. Peters's contacts who reached out. A vet near Missoula. That's where the ranch is. The family vet had been calling as many people in the horse business, breeders, and fellow veterinarians as he could and asking them to put the word out. I'm sorry, honey, but she and her colt have a home, and it's not here."

"Did you even try to buy her?"

"Tim said the family is too distressed right now to discuss anything regarding the ranch or its horses. But from what he understood after talking to the police, apparently Eve escaped during a stop for gas and dinner and the thieves left her behind."

"In the winter? In Montana? And pregnant? Those bastards." Tears she'd been fighting leaked out and trickled down her face. "Does the family know anything about horses? How to take care of them? What they need? Anything?"

He put his arm around her and she sagged against him.

"I'm so sorry. I don't know anything other than the ranch's vet will be here this afternoon to pick them up."

"No. He can't. I'm not ready. It's Sunday. Vets don't work on Sunday."

"I don't have a choice. I have to let them go."

She sniffed. "And Tim is sure Eve is theirs?"

"He's sure. She has impressive papers and is, as we suspected, quite a valuable mare."

Wendy watched Nicholas as he raced around the corral until he finally nuzzled under his mother for milk.

"You stay as long as you want," Zane said. "I'm going to get things ready for her to go."

"When will the truck get here?"

"Sometime after noon. It's a long drive." He jumped down from the fence. "I brought some apples and carrots if you want to feed them to Eve. By the way, her real name is Arabella."

The horse raised her head and flicked her ears at the mention of her name.

"Pretty name. She seems to recognize it."

Zane handed her a paper sack. "Here. You and Eve have a nice visit."

"Arabella," Wendy said and sniffed.

Zane backed away and watched Wendy sitting on the top rail of the slatted fence. She looked like a natural cowgirl with her ass hanging over the wooden board and the heels of her boots caught on a lower rail. Her long blonde hair was in a ponytail that'd been shoved through the opening of a ballcap. She wore his heavy carcoat with a wool scarf draped around her neck. That coat had never looked as good on him as it did on her. Of course, in his opinion, everything looked better on Wendy than anyone else.

He forced himself to turn and walk away. She'd told him over dinner last night that she'd made some decisions about her life and was ready to put those in place. She hadn't told him what she'd decided or what changes she might want to make in her life. He started to ask her what she'd decided and if it involved him— which he'd hoped it did. But he couldn't find the right words to ask without conveying his own strong emotions, something he wasn't sure he was ready to discuss.

However, he was sure he wanted her to stay longer —an undefined length of time—instead of the four days they had remaining. The idea of her not being at the ranch, not sleeping under the same roof, made his stomach hurt and his chest ache, which was interesting since he felt so hollow inside. He'd never been a man comfortable talking about feelings and love. He spoke with actions, not words. Either she didn't get his nonverbal message about how he adored her, or she had and didn't feel the same.

But Wendy was much like Eve, or rather Arabella. Both of them were extremely valuable females who did not belong to Grizzly Bitterroot Ranch. Both had to go home to where families were anxiously awaiting their returns.

He was at the house for lunch when a large truck with an attached horse trailer pulled down his drive. After wiping his hands on his jeans, he went outside to greet the driver.

"Zane Miller?" the guy asked as he climbed down from the truck.

"That's me."

"I'm Dr. Harris Hodges from Missoula. I understand you have Arabella here?"

"I do. I hate to sound suspicious, but can I see some identification and proof you have the right to take her."

"Of course."

The man produced his veterinary and driver's licenses. In addition, he had a notarized statement from the family lawyer confirming permission to take the horse.

"Thanks. I hope you understand my caution."

"I do, and I appreciate it. I spoke with Tim Peters today and he told me how well you've cared for Arabella and her new colt. The family appreciates all you've done and asked me to give you this reward."

Dr. Hodges held out a white envelope. Zane took it and opened it. He studied the fifty-thousand dollar check inside.

"Normally, I wouldn't accept any reward. I only did what any other reputable rancher would. However, I'd like to split this money between my ranch hand who's been caring for Arabella and the gentleman who found her on the road and brought her to the Grizzly Bitterroot. I know they can both use the money and they'll appreciate the family's generosity."

"Excellent."

"You can do me one favor, however. Tell the family that if they decide to sell Arabella and or her colt, I would like first right of refusal. That's the only reward I'd like."

Dr. Hodges nodded. "Will do. Honestly, I don't know what will happen with the ranch. Sally Wilburn, the owner, was an older woman whose husband passed some years back. Her children all live in New York or New Jersey or somewhere out east. As far as I know, none of them are horse people."

"So why didn't they just let me buy the horse and save you from the drive down?"

"From what I've observed, the family is in complete shock right now. I don't think any of them can think straight enough to decide what to do with the ranch or it's livestock."

"What about the other horses stolen that night?"

"They were found in Nevada. Up for sale at a horse auction. Some sharp auctioneer checked for a brand and found it. Notified the local sheriff. The thieves are in custody in Nevada for rustling and murder. Some man and his two sons. Not the brightest bulb in the lamp, if you get my drift. Seems they were from Montana originally and had worked at the Wilburn ranch a few years back."

"What's the name?"

"Owens. Ray Owens. Sons are—"

"Ray, Junior, and Cletus."

"Yeah. You know them?"

"Unfortunately."

"Too bad. They sound like trouble."

"With a capital T. Follow me, and I'll take you to Arabella. Don't mind the cowgirl who's there with them. When she tries to fight you, I'll hold her back."

Dr. Hodges chuckled. "Appreciate it."

Wendy stood in the corral talking to Arabella while feeding her a carrot. If she heard the men approaching, she didn't respond.

"Wendy. Dr. Hodges is here."

"He can't have her," she announced with finality.

"Now, Wendy, honey, we talked about this. You have to let her and the colt go."

Her eyes were red and her face splotchy when she turned around. "I really don't want to."

"I know."

Zane opened the gate and he and Dr. Hodges entered.

It wasn't long before the horses were loaded and headed back to their home.

That evening, Zane pulled a chicken spaghetti casserole from the freezer and put it in the oven to cook. He found Wendy in her room sitting cross-legged on the bed.

"Knock, knock. Can I come in?"

"Sure." She scooted over and patted the mattress. "Have a seat."

He sat on the edge, then swung his legs up and shifted until his back rested on the headboard and his legs were extended.

"You okay?"

"I am." She shook her head with a sad smile. "Amazing how attached you can get to something in such a short time."

Was she talking about the ranch or Arabella and Nicholas? Was it possible she was talking about him?

He nodded. "Or someone."

She laid her head on his shoulder. "True."

"It's hard to not get attached to newborns, be them human or animal."

"True again," she said with a sigh. She lifted her head and looked into his eyes. "But I promise you, I am going to try to buy those horses from the family."

He looked over at her and smiled. "I hope you do."

They sat without speaking for a while until he said, "When I envisioned getting in bed with you, this isn't exactly what I had in mind."

"You thought about me in bed?" She scooted around to face him. "What did you envision?"

"Me. You. Naked. Sex so hot we melted the shingles off the roof."

She nodded. "Melting shingles would take some heat, especially with the snow on them right now."

He chuckled. "You know it, but I had faith in us."

She got quiet, and he wondered what she was thinking.

"So what happened?" she finally asked.

"I don't know. Timing. Circumstances." He smiled. "Crazy exes. The perfect storm to destroy the mood, I guess."

"Well, you know, I might have had a thought or two myself."

"About us? Hot, hot sex?"

She turned a grin his way, and his stomach clenched.

"Maybe." She winked.

He reached for her at the same time a buzzer rang on his phone. He groaned.

"What's that?"

With a sexually frustrated sigh, he pulled his phone from his front pocket. "Timer on the stove," he explained. "Dinner's ready."

"Hmm," she said as she pulled her shirt up and over her head. "Here I was thinking of something other than dinner."

Her creamy, full breasts flowed over the top of a pink lace bra. Her erect nipples poked through the flimsy material.

"Don't move," he ordered as he stood. "Dinner can be reheated."

He raced downstairs, flipped off the oven, and hurried back up, removing his T-shirt on the climb.

She was just where he'd left her. With a smile so wide his cheeks hurt, he leapt onto the bed.

"Now, where were we?"

Chapter Fourteen

He didn't give her time to answer. Suddenly, he was kissing her, running his hand up and down her spine. She felt her bra loosen without even being aware of when he'd undone the clasp.

She latched her fingers under the straps, pulled the bra off, and tossed it somewhere. Right now, she didn't care where it landed. He pulled her tight, her breasts flattening against his hard, muscular chest. She rubbed her aching nipples in his rough chest hair and groaned at the sweet pleasure.

He broke the kiss, moving his lips to her neck and down to her shoulder. She cocked her head to the side to give him better access and encouragement to keep going. With bites and nibbles, soothed with his lips and tongue, he worked his way over her shoulder and down her chest.

"Oh, baby," he cooed, kissing one nipple and then the other. "So beautiful. So sexy," he muttered before his mouth covered the tip of one breast while his fingers pinched the other. He tugged the nipple deep into his mouth, and she squirmed from the decadent lightning zapping her sex. The area between her thighs throbbed with need and desire.

They were both adults. Both knew where this would end, and right now, she wanted him to move it along faster before she erupted into flames and burned the house down.

She ran her heel up and down the back of his leg and then wrapped it around his thigh. She ground against his leg, trying to massage her growing twinge.

"God, Zane. I love that."

At her words, he moved his mouth to the other breast and applying even greater suction, pulled it deeper, tonguing her swollen flesh. At the same time, he pinched the other nipple firmly, causing her hips to lift off the bed.

Her hands fisted in his hair and pulled at the strands. She pushed the back of her head into the mattress with a guttural moan.

And then his mouth slid to her abdomen, his tongue rimming her navel and then flicking in the hole. She raked her fingernails down his back.

"Off," she ordered. "Everything off."

He ignored her demand, and instead, he untied her lounging pants and thrust his hand inside.

"Are you wet for me, Wendy? Are you as turned on as I am?" His fingers found the waist of her panties and slipped inside. "Oh, you are," he said in a husky voice. "But I already knew that. The aroma of your arousal has me hard as a hammer."

"Good," she said on a breathy voice. "I definitely have a nail that needs a pounding."

He chuckled. "Oh, babe, I've been dying for another taste of you. Once wasn't enough."

Climbing off the bed, he stripped her pants and panties as he went. As soon as her clothes hit the floor, he spread her legs and latched his mouth onto her sensitive flesh.

Her hips rose off the bed in response. He slid his hands under her elevated ass and held her firmly to his mouth. He drank and sucked and licked her until she thought she would die. Instead, her climax hit like a tornado, shattering her into a million pieces.

When she finally stopped shaking, he looked up at her from between her thighs.

"We've only just begun," he said.

"Is that a warning or a promise?"

He smiled, and one full wall surrounding her heart collapsed.

"Maybe a little of both."

He stood and stripped. His toned body was an artistic work of muscular curves and dips. Her mouth salivated at the vision.

She crooked her finger. "Come here."

He walked to the bed, but she stopped him before he got back on the mattress.

"Your turn for a little torture."

She flicked out her tongue and ran it in the groove from his waist to his groin.

He sucked in his breath.

She wrapped her lips around the head of his cock and sucked. His fingers sunk into her hair.

With as much suction as she could manage, she pulled his dick into her mouth until he hit the back of her throat. Then, she slowly slid it back out, raking her teeth gently along the thick vein.

"Nope. Sorry," he said pulling her mouth off him. "I'm afraid I have a cocked and loaded...well, cock. I want to be inside you. I want to feel your soft walls surround me. I want to come inside you. If you continue using your sweet, sweet mouth on me, it'll all be over before I'm ready."

She lay back and opened her arms. "I want you inside me, too."

He pulled a condom from his jeans and slipped it on. And then he was back and pushing and stretching her to accommodate his girth. He filled her. Not just her canal, but black holes inside her she didn't want to acknowledge.

With each stroke, she climbed higher and higher until a wave broke over her. Her muscles shook with each jolt of orgasmic electricity flowing through her.

He followed closely behind, calling her name gently in her ear. "Wendy. Wendy. Dear Wendy."

Thirty minutes passed before either of them found the energy to go downstairs for dinner. She didn't bother with panties and clothing since she suspected those would be a waste of time...both putting them on and him taking them back off. She put on her robe and warm Ugg houseshoes and followed him downstairs.

"I'll reheat if you get the fire going," she suggested.

"You've got a deal."

She carried two plates of spaghetti and two beers into the living room where a blazing fire warmed the room. They sat on the thick rug in front of the hearth to eat.

"Do you have to go?" he asked.

"I need to go."

She didn't want to go. The weeks here had been invaluable. She'd had the time and the space to think about her past and look to what she wanted her future to be. She was pretty sure she knew what she wanted, but to be absolutely certain, she had to go home.

The longer she stayed, the more difficult it would be to leave him and the ranch. In her heart she knew what she had to do and she was positive that the sooner she left, the better. Telling him good bye now would be painful. A month from now, leaving him would be damned near impossible.

Besides, asking if she had to go wasn't the same as asking her to stay. For her to stay, he would have to say the words.

"I thought you were really enjoying Montana."

"I am. I love it. This place, the people, have been wonderful. They have welcomed me like I've lived here my whole life. Edie, well, what can I say? She's become the friend I didn't know I needed."

"If you stay, you'll get to see her new baby. And Lori's baby. You'd have two newborns to play with."

She chuckled. "I have a nephew at home waiting to get to know his aunt. But I am sorry I won't get to see those babies."

"Then stay. I'll keep you working. Heck, I know you don't need the money, but I'll put you on the payroll so you're not on vacation."

The smile that came to her lips was sad. He couldn't simply tell her that he wanted her to stay. Instead, everything he offered was about the ranch and money. She didn't have to have either of those. All she wanted was him, but he hadn't offered her that.

"You're making it so hard." She leaned forward and kissed him. "Thank you. I'm so glad I got to know you."

He pulled her closer and wrapped both arms around her. "You sound like you're leaving tonight."

"Not tonight, but soon."

They left the dirty dishes in the kitchen and headed back to bed. She had a lifetime of memories to make and a short time to make them.

The next morning, Zane woke her with kisses and tender lovemaking. When he finally left the bed, he said, "Take it easy today. We have a late night of partying scheduled."

She nodded and pulled him back down for a deep kiss.

"Honey, you keep that up, and Albert won't get his carrots today."

With a deep inhale and sigh, she released him.

"Well, I wouldn't want to make Albert unhappy." She pushed him away with her foot. "Go. Get."

He kissed her again. "See you later."

She smiled with a nod.

As soon as he was gone, she made two phone calls. First for the plane, and the second to Edie.

"Can you come pick me up?"

"Sure. Where do you need to go?"

"I'll tell you on the way. Can you be here by nine?"

"Sure."

Edie pulled into the drive about a quarter to nine. Wendy waited on the front porch with her luggage.

"What's going on?" Edie asked.

"I'll explain. Pop the hatch please."

Wendy loaded her bags and climbed into the passenger seat. "My dad has sent the plane for me. It'll meet us at the Gardiner airport. Can you take me there please?"

Edie's mouth pinched. "And if I say no, then what?"

"I'll start trying to find an Uber in the area."

Edie huffed and started her car. "You have some explaining to do. I can't believe you're going to miss the party tonight." She huffed out a breath. "Talk."

On the drive, Wendy told her everything. The breathtaking kisses. The long talks at night in front of the fireplace. The rides disguised as exercise. The jokes. The laughs. Christmas Eve. And finally, last night.

"And I know the longer I stay, the more my leaving

will hurt. I decided to use the Band-Aid method. Rip it off fast."

Edie clicked her tongue. "You have fallen in love with Zane."

"I never said that."

"Sure you did. Do you even listen to yourself?" She scoffed. "I never saw you as a coward, Wendy. I'm so disappointed."

"You're wrong. Leaving is the hardest thing I've ever done. Zane is happy here. This is his family home. He has plans for his future. I just don't have a place in them. In the long run, this will be the best for both of us."

"I'm going to call the Chicago bitch as soon as I get home and tell her that he's back on the market."

Wendy laughed. "Knock yourself out. He made it quite clear to her that they were done."

Edie gave a loud sigh. "I had such plans for us, you know?" She looked over at Wendy. "You were going to marry Zane, and then you and I would become besties. You'd be there for my delivery and when my kids got sick, I'd have a good friend who happened to be a doctor who would tell me what to do."

"Got my future all planned, huh? Sorry. But there's nothing to prevent you from flying down to Dallas to see me. There are tons of places to shop and fabulous restaurants for dining and the shows. Broadway plays all the time. I could take you everywhere. We would have so much fun."

Edie patted her extended belly. "I'll be a mom to two soon. Frank and his brother work hard and do everything possible to make the ranch a success. But money is tight. Leaving my two young children with their dad who already has too much to do, well, I don't see that happening."

Edie turned onto the Gardiner airport's gravel drive and pulled to a stop near the runway. A tear rolled down her cheek. "I don't think I'll ever see you again, Wendy, and that makes me sad."

Wendy hugged her. "This isn't goodbye. I swear. We'll talk on the phone like we've been doing. I'll come back and visit."

"Hey, you're a big-time, fancy doctor. You'll jump back into your world and your life will get crazy busy again."

Through the windshield, Wendy watched her family plane roll to a stop. Her heart wanted to argue with Edie, swear that she'd stay in touch after she got home. But her head? No, her head knew that Edie was probably right. This was more than likely the end.

"Thank you, Edie."

"For what? Giving you a way to run away?"

"For being my friend. For listening to me. For giving me a ride today. And I'm only going to say this once and never again. I do love Zane and that's why I'm leaving."

She climbed from the SUV and unloaded her bags. The pilot stowed them as she climbed the stairs. At the door, she turned back and waved. Edie blinked her headlights twice, turned her car around, and drove away.

Wendy found her seat and buckled in for the flight back to her life.

ZANE FINISHED WORK EARLY AND HEADED TO THE house to shower for the party tonight. He needed to leave time to pick up whatever Wendy wanted to drink. Whatever else he bought for the party, he wanted to make sure he had a bottle of champagne. Tonight, he was going to tell her how he felt about her. He hadn't been looking for love, but it had sneaked up on him and booted him in the ass.

He grinned. His heart swelled with love every time he thought about Wendy. She was special. Unique. Interesting. He didn't think they could ever run out of things to talk about, and seeing as he had plans for her that involved the rest of his life, not running out of talking topics would be convenient.

Were his good pair of jeans clean? Gosh, had he thrown them in the laundry the last time he'd worn them? He couldn't remember. What shirt for tonight? Maybe he'd look for one with snaps for fast removal later.

He was whistling as he bounded up the stairs. Opening the door to the house, he called, "Wendy? You here?"

He toed off his boots and left them on the enclosed porch. His gaze fell on the empty peg where Wendy had been hanging her coat.

"Wendy?" he called again. "Where are you?"

There was no fire to greet him. Only embers on

their last gasps. No casserole in the oven. No television running. No beautiful blonde in the living room reading a book.

"Wendy?" he called up the stairs. He took the steps two at a time. She was probably in the shower or just out of the shower and couldn't hear him.

When he knocked on her bedroom door, it swung open. The bed was made. The closet door was closed. The four suitcases that'd been lined up along the walls were gone. The room was as neat as he'd ever seen it. It was as if Wendy had never existed, never been in this room. Except she had. Her scent remained, but that was all.

His room was as he'd left it. Bed unmade. Jeans thrown over a chair.

The bathroom was spotless. No wet towels. No damp shower mat.

Downstairs again, he finally saw the piece of paper fluttering on the refrigerator. Even from a distance, he recognized her handwriting. He knew what it said without reading it. Oh, not the specific words but the message. Still, he had to see for himself.

Dear Zane,

Thank you for the most incredible three weeks of my life. I didn't realize how much I'd missed my family's ranch until I shared your home. I can't begin to thank you for opening your door to a stranger and making her feel like she was home.

And thank you for sharing your friends with me. They welcomed me with open arms. For that, I'll always be grateful.

I know you will be mad that I left, but I realized after last night that the longer I was here, the more leaving will hurt. I don't do this lightly. I know you have plans for your future, wonderful and exciting plans. I know you and Eli will build a successful dude ranch. I will pray for his safe return.

Know that our time together will always hold a special place in my heart. I will never forget you or Grizzly Bitterroot Ranch.

All my love,

Wendy

He stumbled backward, ran into a stool, and sat.

This must be what it feels like to be gut shot, he thought. The pain exploding inside was almost unbearable. His stomach clenched. He pressed his hand over the pain. The intense ache did not abate. He was in agony.

As the concrete realization that she'd really left hit him, his head spun.

He grabbed an unopened bottle of bourbon and headed to the living room. Being dumped deserved a good drunk, right? Maybe he could stop his brain from reeling and numb the pain in his heart and his gut. He cracked open the top and took a long gulp. The first one didn't help, but maybe the next ten or so might.

New Year's Day started with a blinding headache. The ache from the flu couldn't hold a candle to the ache from his empty heart.

As he made his way down the aisle in the east wing of the barn, he passed stall five. He stopped and looked in the vacant space. Funny how some animals, and some people, could crawl inside a man's heart and take root before he was even aware what was happening.

Wendy and Arabella. Two beautiful queens who'd both returned to their rightful homes.

He sighed and hefted the handles of a wheelbarrow full of horse manure and began pushing it to the trailer where he'd load it to haul over to his mother's garden for next year. And when he was done with that load, he'd do it again and again and again until he didn't notice the hole Wendy had left in his chest.

Chapter Fifteen

"**D**r. McCool. We've got a dog bite in the emergency department that needs your special touch," the medical resident on the phone said.

Wendy sighed and looked at her full schedule. "Why me?"

"She's a model. Asked specifically for you."

"Okay. I'll be there as soon as I can."

"Sandy," Wendy called as soon as she hung up the phone. "I need to run to the ER to stitch up some prima donna's face. Can you make a hole in my schedule?"

Her nurse's head popped through the door. "No can do. Sorry, boss. You've got four rhinoplasties, and two breast augmentations already waiting in exam rooms. After those, you've got four post-ops to see."

Wendy had been home for three weeks and she was right back on the hamster wheel, running and running, but this time, she was moving forward instead of jogging in place.

"Crap. Can you turf the post-ops to Amy?"

The growing practice had recently added Amy Milan, an experienced physician assistant, to their staff.

"Let me check." Sandy disappeared back into the hall.

Wendy headed into the first of her four rhino-plasty pre-operative examinations.

It close to two hours before she found a gap in her schedule that allowed her to head to the emergency room. Margery Walls, a long-time patient, sat in a bed talking on the phone. She held up one finger when Wendy walked in.

"Off the phone now, or I'm gone."

"Just a minute." Margery covered the phone with her hand. "This is important. This is my agent."

"Margery, I don't care if that's Jesus on the phone. I have patients waiting on me."

The model huffed. "I've got to go, Jerry. I'll call you back." She slipped the phone into her purse as Wendy washed her hands. "If you weren't so damned good at this, I'd go to a nicer doctor."

Wendy shrugged. "I gave you a list of new doctors last month."

"No. You're the best." She rolled her stunning, jade-green eyes. "Just fix my face."

Wendy removed the four-by-four inch bandage and studied the break in the flesh. The bite would require maybe two stitches. It was far from serious, but

Margery's face was worth millions, so she cleaned the area and got to work placing micro stitches.

That evening, Wendy poured herself a double serving of red wine and headed over to her sister's condo. She found Risa in her son's room changing a dirty diaper.

"Room smells like poop," Wendy said, leaning on the doorframe.

"Don't listen to your Aunt Wendy. She's the poop-head around here."

"Hey. I was kidding."

Risa picked up her son and turned around. "No, you weren't. You've been negative and snarly since you got home. I was hoping those weeks away would have soothed your temper."

Wendy sighed. "I know."

"Follow me onto the sunporch. While I feed Stephen, tell me what bug has bitten your ass."

"Not a bug," Wendy said, following behind her sister. "It's just…"

"Just what?" Risa sat in a rocking chair and put her son to her breast. "It can't be still about Mae and the whole Roy debacle. That's dead news, especially since Mae is engaged again."

Wendy sat and chuckled. "Our cousin wasted no time, did she?"

"Well, when it's right, it's right."

Wendy's heart jabbed her at Risa's words.

"And that's exactly what you felt as soon as Trevor reentered your life?"

"I'd never admit this to him, but, yes. When I saw

him after so many years apart, I swear my heart sighed and said, 'Where have you been?'"

Wendy took a large gulp of wine. Her heart had been doing a lot of talking to her since she'd returned to Dallas.

"Seriously, Wendy? You're drinking that wine like it's water."

"The more I drink, the faster I go to sleep."

"Now that's just wrong on every level. I'm worried about you. What happened in Montana anyway? Every time I called, you were headed out to the barn, or eating dinner, or doing something that necessitated you not being on the phone. And since you've been back, you've ignored every attempt I've made to talk about it. Was your trip that bad? From what little you've said, it sounded like you had a good break from work."

"No. It wasn't bad at all." Wendy set her glass on the coffee table. "I'm thirty-five years old. I have an incredible career, a fabulous condo, nice clothes, and a handsome nephew I adore. I feel like an almost completed puzzle except for that piece that goes dead center that would complete the picture."

Risa nodded. "I see." She smiled. "You fell in love while you were gone."

Wendy sighed and nodded. "I thought so while I was there, but I had to come home to know for sure." She sighed again. "It's true. I've finally fall in love and it sucks. I thought he was feeling it, too, and hoped that some time apart would help him realize it, but I haven't heard from Zane since I've been back."

"Ah. Zane Miller. Mom's friend's son."

"Well, yeah. Who did you think I was talking about?"

Risa smiled. "I was hoping it wasn't Roy Livingston."

Wendy laughed. "If you weren't holding my favorite person in the whole world, I would tickle you until you cried uncle or wet your pants."

Her sister snickered. "Speaking of Roy, I heard through the grapevine that he's dating that Carr girl."

"Which one? Cara or Carla?"

"Carla, I think. Anyway, back to Zane."

"No, there's no back to Zane. I realized while I was there that what I wanted was a different type of medical practice. I love helping people who really need me. I want to be done with the vanity surgeries and it's taken most of the month I've been back to accomplish that. I know some doctors quit their practices and walk out, but I'd never do that to my partners, so I'm winding down and transferring my patients to other doctors in the practice. I've been investigating general surgery or a family practice in a small community where my surgical skills would be an asset."

"Sort of like Gardiner, Montana?"

Wendy frowned. "Maybe. I thought about Gardiner a lot while I was there. I loved the feeling of community, of people helping each other." She took a sip of wine. "You know, you'd think if Zane had any interest in pursuing me, he would have reached out by now."

"And you haven't reached out to him because?"

"Because he already has one crazy, clingy ex. I don't want to even begin to appear like that. I think he has to make the first move."

"Does he feel the same for you as you feel for him?"

"I thought he did, or he was beginning to, but his silence since I left speaks volumes, don't you think?"

"Not necessarily. Trevor and I didn't speak for years, but neither of us fell out of love with the other. Our timing wasn't right back then. Maybe your problem is the same. The time isn't right yet."

"I don't know. I'm not a kid any more. I feel like my life is speeding along at a hundred miles per hour. We'll be forty before we know it."

"Hold on, sis. Don't age us faster than we already are."

Wendy chuckled. "You know what I mean."

"Yes, I do. Look, all I can say is I thought I had everything until Trevor walked back into my life and I realized my life and everything associated with it was a thousand—no, a million times better when I had Trevor to share it with. If something happened to him or Stephen, or if they weren't in my life, I wouldn't be the person I am." She smiled. "You look confused. What I'm trying to say, and not doing a good job of it, is that it's the love I share with those two that changed me, made me see life in a different light."

"And I'm happy for you, but I'm not sure I'm in the same place."

"So call Zane. Talk to him. Feel him out. Maybe

he's as miserable to be around as you are."

Wendy stuck out her tongue. "Ha ha. You're so funny."

Risa laughed. "You're unhappy here. It's been obvious since you came home. I suspect you left your heart in Montana."

"If I did, I may have to learn to live without it."

"Damnit, Russ. I told you I wanted you to exercise Belle today, not Albert."

Cowboy Russ looked at Zane. "Man, you've got to get that woman back. You're damned near impossible to live with."

"I can fire you," Zane warned.

"Naw. I work for your dad, and he likes me." Russ slapped Zane's back. "Call the woman. Tell her you're in love with her and beg her to come back."

"I never said I was in love with Wendy," Zane huffed.

"And I never said Wendy, now did I?" He clicked his tongue, and he and Bella walked out of the barn and down the drive.

Damn him. Did Russ think Zane could just ring up Wendy after three weeks and tell her he loved her and she'd jump on a plane and fly back? Ridiculous. Who would want to move from Dallas, where she has everything available to her, to a tiny town like Gardiner? She's a plastic surgeon. He was out of his mind if he thought for one minute she would give up her practice.

He was still stewing when his cell phone rang. The displayed number was in Montana but unfamiliar.

"Zane Miller."

"Mr. Miller. This is Dr. Hodges from Missoula. Do you remember me?"

"Of course. How is Arabella and her colt?"

"Both are doing very well. The family kept the name Nicholas since he was born on Christmas Eve."

Zane smiled, the first real smile he'd felt on his face in three long weeks. "Glad to hear it. What can I do for you?"

"Well, I think it's what I can do for you that will interest you."

It took Zane two days to get everything he needed in place. The last step were the pictures he shot of Arabella and Nicholas in their corral. Then he sat down at his computer to write the hardest letter he'd ever written. Not that the words were difficult, but laying his feelings out so openly was a risk. This might work, and it might not, but he had nothing to lose and everything to gain.

He popped the top on a beer, took a long swig, and fired up his computer.

Dear Wendy,

I'll warn you now that I'm better with numbers than emotions and words.

The last three weeks haven't been the same around the ranch. Oh, the horses are doing fine. Russ and Lori continue as before, although Lori's getting big as a house (but don't tell her I said that. Pregnant women can get mean!) Edie and Sheila ask about you, and when I say I haven't talked to you,

*both women slug my arm. I have bruises on both arms.
I swear.*

*But the house is too quiet. No one is singing off-key in the
shower except me. The casseroles and groceries that Lori provides
last too long because there's only me to eat them. Pike and Coda
looked for you after you left. I found Coda in your old room on
your bed last week, and that's not like her. She misses you.*

Coda isn't the only one.

*I miss you. I miss your laugh. Your horrible pun jokes. Your
feet propped on the hearth warming your toes while you read the
latest, best-selling romance novel. I miss your touch. Your scent. I
miss your face when you've forced yourself out of bed and you're
still half-asleep. I miss hearing you talking to Albert about
growing up. I miss your little snore when you fall asleep when
we're watching a movie. Worst of all, I miss your kisses, how
you tasted, and how you made me feel stronger and more alive
than I ever have.*

When you left, you took my heart with you.

*I love you, Wendy. I need you in my life. If not here in
Montana, then I'll come to you.*

*I'll do anything in my power to make you happy. I've
attached two new purchases for the ranch. They miss you, too.*

Come home to me or I'll come to you. Just say the word.

All my love,

Zane

He hit send and leaned back in his chair. He'd
made his serve. The ball was in her court.

Twenty-four hours passed without a reply. Then
thirty-six, forty-eight, and then seventy-two.

He'd waited too long, or he'd horribly misread her.

A week after he sent his email, a large delivery

truck pulled into his drive. The driver hopped out with a clipboard in his hand.

"This Grizzly Bitterroot?" he asked.

"Yup," Zane said.

"Sign here."

"I didn't order anything."

"Don't know nothing except I was told to deliver this here and get a signature."

Zane shrugged and signed on the line.

"Thanks," the driver said. He slid the back of his truck open and pulled a large, brown moving box from inside. "Where do you want them?"

"Them?"

"These boxes."

"How many are there?"

"Twenty."

"Twenty? What the heck is in them?"

Before the driver could answer, Edie's SUV rolled into the drive, her horn honking the whole way.

Zane stepped from behind the truck to wave at Edie. But it wasn't Edie's vehicle. It was a brand-new SUV he didn't recognize. He squinted and studied the woman behind the wheel. His heart jumped into his throat. The SUV parked next to his truck. He hurried over and jerked the door open. Wendy looked up at him and smiled.

"I hope you were serious in your note."

He pulled her from the car and wrapped his arms around her. "Of course I was serious." He kissed her. She was perfect in his arms. "Why didn't you answer?"

"I am. I'm doing it right now." She leaned forward and kissed him again. "My answer is yes, I love you. Yes, I want to be with you, too. Yes, I missed you. Did you know it's a long freaking drive from Dallas to here?"

"You drove?"

"Well how else am I going to get my new four-wheel drive SUV that's perfect for nasty winter weather and all my clothes here?"

"Mister? Did you decide where you want these boxes?" the driver called to him.

"You're here? To stay?"

"I'm here to stay. I hope that's okay with you."

"More than okay. I love you, Wendy. But what about your practice? Your family? Your condo?"

She grabbed his face and kissed him. "My sister tells me I'm a miserable person to be around, or at least I have been since I left you. She helped me pack, but she sent you a warning."

He grinned. "What's that?"

"If you hurt her sister, her husband is ex-military and no one will ever find your body."

He laughed. "She's kidding, right?"

Wendy shrugged and then grinned. "I'll protect you from my big, bad brother-in-law."

"And your parents?"

"Hated to see me go, but was thrilled I'd found the man of my dreams."

"The man of your dreams. I like that." He gave her a side eye. "That's me, right? I don't want to presume."

She laughed. "Of course it is, you idiot. You are the perfect man for me."

"Whew. I was worried you might be speaking of Albert or Nicholas."

She lifted an eyebrow. "Well, you do make a strong point for your competition,"

He hugged her and made her giggle.

"But, what about your practice?"

"Gone. Finished. I quit."

"What?"

"Gave my notice the day I got home. It's taken me most of the month to clear my calendar and transfer my patients to other physicians. I was kind of hoping there was a small town in Montana that might like to have a part-time doctor-part-time-cowgirl."

"I can think of one Montana cowboy who loves that idea."

"I know a part-time-doctor-part-time-cowgirl who is mighty happy to hear that."

Zane slid his arm around her waist and they walked back to the house. The boxes and Wendy would go to his room for now. Building their new house had just jumped to the top of his to-do list.

"Tell me the truth. You came back for Arabella, Nicholas, and Albert, didn't you?" he joked.

"Naw," she said and kissed his cheek. "Their emails weren't nearly as persuasive as yours."

He laughed and hugged her, and that's when he saw their future. Hugs and laughter. They were going to have a wonderful life together.

About the Author

New York Times and USA Today Bestselling Author Cynthia D'Alba was born and raised in a small Arkansas town. After being gone for a number of years, she's thrilled to be making her home back in Arkansas living on the banks of an eight-thousand acre lake.

Photo by Annie Ray

When she's not reading or writing or plotting, she's doorman for her spoiled border collie, cook, housekeeper and chief bottle washer for her husband and slave to a noisy, messy parrot. She loves to chat online with friends and fans.

Send snail mail to: Cynthia D'Alba PO Box 2116 Hot Springs, AR 71914

Or better yet! She would for you to take her newsletter. She promises not to spam you, not to fill your inbox with advertising, and not to sell your name and email address to anyone. Check her website for a link to her newsletter.

www.cynthiadalba.com
https://cynthiadalba.com/newsletter-sign-up/
cynthiadalba@gmail.com

facebook.com/cynthiadalba

twitter.com/cynthiadalba

bookbub.com/profile/cynthia-d-alba

goodreads.com/CynthiaDAlba

amazon.com/Cynthia-DAlba

instagram.com/cynthiadalba

Keep reading for excerpts from other
Dallas Debutante books.

Hot SEAL, Black Coffee
A Dallas Debutante/SEALs in Paradise/McCool
Trilogy (Book 1)

*Dealing with a sexy ex-girlfriend, a jewel heist,
and a murder-for-hire can make an ex-SEAL
bodyguard a tad cranky.*

Trevor Mason accepts what should be a simple
job…protect the jewels his ex-girlfriend will wear to a
breast cancer fundraiser. As founder and owner of Eye
Spy International, he should send one of his guys, but
he needs to get his ex out of his system and this is the
perfect opportunity to remind himself that she is a
spoiled, rich debutante who dumped him with a Dear
John letter during his SEAL training.

Respected breast cancer doctor Dr. Risa McCool
hates being in the limelight for her personal life. Her
life's work is breast cancer treatment and research,
which she'd rather be known for than for her carefree,
partying debutante years. She agrees to be the chair-

person for the annual breast cancer fundraiser even though it means doing publicity appearances and interviews, all while wearing the famous pink Breast Cancer Diamond for each public event. The multi-million dollar value of the pink stone requires an armed bodyguard at all times.

Past attractions flame, proving to be a distraction to the serious reality of the situation. When Risa and the millions in diamonds go missing, nothing will stop Trevor from bringing her home, with or without the jewels.

At two-thirty Monday afternoon, Dr. Risa McCool's world shifted on its axis. He was back. She wasn't ready. But then, would she ever be ready?

Four hours passed before she was able to disengage from work and go home. As she pulled under the portico of her high-rise building and the condo valet hurried out to park her eight-year-old sedan, her stomach roiled at the realization that Trevor Mason—high school and college boyfriend and almost fiancé—would be waiting for her in her condo, or at least should be. She pressed a shaking hand to her abdomen and inhaled a deep, calming breath. It didn't work. There was still a slight quiver to her hands as she grabbed her purse and briefcase from the passenger seat.

She paused to look in the mirror. A tired brunette looked back at her. Dark circles under her eyes. Limp hair pulled into a ponytail at the back of her head. Pale lips. Paler cheeks. Not one of her better looks.

Would he be the same? Tall with sun-kissed hair and mesmerizing azure-blue eyes?

Tall, sure. That was a given.

Eye color would have to be the same, but his sun-bleached hair? His muscular physique? In high school and college, he'd played on the offense for their high school and college football teams, but she had never really understood what he did. Sometimes he ran and sometimes he hit other guys. What she remembered were strong arms and a wide chest. Would those be the same?

Almost fifteen years had passed since she'd last seen him. He hadn't come back for their tenth nor their fifteenth high school reunions. The explanation for his absences involved SEAL missions to who knew where. Risa had wondered if she'd ever see him again, whether he'd make it through all his deployments and secret ops.

Well, he had and now she had to work with him.

She took a deep breath and slid from the car.

"Good Evening, Dr. McCool," the valet said.

"Evening, John. Do you know if my guest arrived?"

"Yes, ma'am. About four hours ago."

"Do you know if the groceries were delivered?"

"Yes, ma'am. Cleaning service has also been in."

"Thank you. Have a nice evening."

"You, too."

She acknowledged the guard on duty at the desk with a nod and continued to the private residents-only elevator that opened to a back-door entrance to her condo. After putting her key in the slot, she pressed the button for the forty-first floor and then leaned against the wall for the ride.

Her anxiety at seeing Trevor climbed as the elevator dinged past each floor. It was possible, even probable, that she had made a mistake following her mother's advice to employ his company. She was required to have a bodyguard for every public event since the announcement of the pink Breast Cancer Diamond. Her insurance company insisted on it. The jewelry designer demanded it. And worse, her mother was adamant on a guard. How did one say no to her mother?

Plus, as head of the Dallas Area Breast Cancer Research Center, she'd been tasked with wearing that gaudy necklace with a pink diamond big enough to choke a horse for the annual fundraising gala. The damn thing was worth close to fifteen or twenty million and was heavy as hell. Who'd want it?

The elevator dinged one last time and the doors slid open. She stepped into a small vestibule and let herself into her place expecting to see Trevor.

Only, she didn't.

Instead there was music—jazz to be specific. She

followed the sounds of Stan Getz to her balcony, her heart in her throat.

A man sat in a recliner facing the night lights of Dallas, a highball in one hand, a cigar in the other.

"I'm glad to see you stock the good bourbon," he said, lifting the glass, but not turning to face her. "And my brand, too. Should I be impressed?"

Her jaw clenched. Their fights had always been about money—what she had and what he didn't.

"I don't know," she said. "Are you impressed?"

He took a drag off the cigar and chased the smoke down his throat with a gulp of hundred-dollar bourbon. "Naw. You can afford it."

"Are you going to look at me or will my first conversation with you in fifteen years be with the back of your head?"

After stabbing out the cigar, he finished his drink, sat it on the tile floor, and rose. Lord, he was still as towering and overwhelming as she remembered him. At five-feet-ten-inches, Risa was tall, but Trevor's height made her feel positively petite. As he turned, every muscle in her body tensed as she stood unsure whether she was preparing to fight him, flee from him or fuck him.

"Hello, Risa."

Christmas in His Arms
Dallas Debutante/McCool Trilogy (Book 2)

My name is Opal Mae McCool. I love my parents, but
that name? Ugh, but I've adjusted. This year has been
rocking along until October when my entire life lands
in the toilet and someone flushes. First, my groom
dumps me at the altar. Confession…not as destroyed
as I should have been. Then, I share a steamy kiss with
old love which leads to…nothing. Radio silence. Fine.
Disappointed, but moving on. However, it's almost
Christmas and I make a quick overnight business trip
to Montana just in time for the snowmageddon and
I'm stuck in Bozeman with only clean panties and a
toothbrush. Next year has to be better, right?

I'm Michael Rockland. Born, raised and will die in
Texas and I'm fine with that. I'm a mechanic at heart,
even if my everyday job doesn't allow me under the
hood. About a month ago, I discovered I'm the Friday
Lunch Special at a local diner. I'd be pissed if it wasn't

for a good cause and it hadn't led me back to the love of my life. One hot, steamy kiss, a promise for the future, and she shuts me out. Harsh, but I'm a big boy. I can deal with reality, except when she ends up on my grandparents' doorstep in Montana.

My dad doesn't approve of him. His mother doesn't approve of me. It's not quite the Capulets and Montagues, and we are long past the teenage years, so isn't it time to let us decide if we belong together or not?

"You look stunning."

I glanced into the mirror as my cousin Wendy adjusted my bridal veil. With skepticism, I met her gaze in the reflection.

"I'm serious," Wendy said. "You've never looked more radiant than you do at this moment, well, except maybe the night of your debutante presentation. You were radiant that evening."

"And the good thing about my wedding is I don't have to fear the Dallas Debutante Dip." I laughed even as a shiver of fear ran down my spine at the memory of learning, and performing, the graceful curtsey that took every Dallas Debutante downward, close enough that her forehead could touch the floor, or at least should, if done properly. Thank goodness for my big hair that night. I'd faked the floor touch without anyone knowing. Whew.

"I don't know why you two go on and on about that silly bow. It wasn't that difficult," her other cousin Risa said.

Wendy turned to look at her twin sister. "You couldn't do the dip at this moment if your life depended on it."

Risa giggled as she placed both her hands on her protruding, and very pregnant, belly. "I believe you have a valid point. I can barely stand from sitting. Getting up from the floor would be impossible."

"Without a crane," her sister quipped.

As I watched my twin cousins take playful jabs at each other, I envied their tight relationship. As an only child, I'd been blessed with every possible advantage in life. Money. Great parents. Excellent education. Passable looks.

Yep, every advantage as long as you didn't consider my name. I mean, I was proud to be named after my great-grandmothers, but growing up I would've given anything to be a Tiffany, or Dawn, or plain ole Mary. Still, no one called me Opal, or Opal Mae, or Opal Mae McCool—unless they were family or trying to pull my chain. To all my friends, I was simply Mae.

"You know what?" I said, swiveling on the stool to face my maid and matron of honor. "I envy you two."

"Us?" Wendy said.

"Why?" Risa asked at the same time.

"You've always had each other, watched out for

each other. I always wished I'd had a sister like one of you."

"Aw, honey," Wendy said, putting her arm around my shoulders "You say that now, but Risa was hell to grow up with. All my boyfriends wanted to date her, and when they couldn't, took me instead."

Risa laughed. "That is not true. Don't listen to her, Mae."

I chuckled. "See? I missed having someone to argue with."

Wendy grew serious. "Weren't we mostly around for you growing up? I mean, we tried to be, didn't we, Risa?"

Risa nodded. "Since we were five when you were born, you were like the best doll we ever had."

"Mom said you two carried me everywhere. Tried to dress me up and push me in a carriage." I smiled at the memory. Risa and Wendy had always been a part of my life, like big sisters who didn't live in my house but were always there when I needed them.

"I remember begging our mom to take us over to Aunt Alice and Uncle Gordon's house to play," Risa said sighing.

A knock at the door interrupted their chatter, and the wedding planner's head popped into the opening. "You ready? It's time."

I rose and drew in a deep breath, trying to calm my nerves. I was getting married and was scared to death, but every bride feels the same way on her wedding day, right? "I'm ready." I heard the quiver in my voice.

Wendy was the only one who really understood what my future as a Livingston might entail. She laid a hand on my shoulder. "Nervous?"

I shrugged. "A little. Marrying into the Livingston family is a big deal." I crossed my fingers and held them up. "Wish me luck."

Wendy hugged me. "Oh, honey. You don't need luck. You have love. The whole Livingston family adores you. Roy is the one who's lucky to have found you."

"You think?" I press my hands against my quivering stomach. "I hope so. Without you, I surely wouldn't be standing here today."

"Maybe I pushed a little for a first date, but after that, it was all you." Wendy laid her head against the side of mine.

"Still, I can't believe all the things you did to help him get ready for the wedding. The tux fittings. Getting his hair styled." I held out my arm and a thick, diamond-encrusted bracelet sparkled in the late afternoon light. "Picking out this incredible diamond bracelet as my wedding present."

Wendy feigned surprised. "How do you know I picked out that bracelet? Maybe Roy did it all on his own."

I gave a little snort. "Yeah, I don't think so. He's not that versed in jewelry."

Wendy scrunched her nose. "Well, maybe I helped him a little."

"I heard his bachelor party was a huge hit," Risa said. "Trevor said you did a great job setting that up."

Wendy shrugged. "I felt for Roy. With Everett gone so much, it's not like his best man could help out, and someone had to do it." She grinned. "And I know for a fact there were no strippers."

My dad stepped into the room and tapped the face of his watch. "Let's move it, ladies. Don't want to be late for the wedding."

"Not like they'll start without me," I joked, but that nervous quiver still shook in my throat. I took my dad's arm. "It's now or never. Lead on."

Dad and I stood out of sight from the opened double doors and watched as Risa made her way down the aisle as my matron of honor. I had to smile at her pregnant waddle, her floral bouquet not beginning to cover her protruding abdomen.

Wendy glided down the rose-petal-strewn carpet as though she were walking on air. I loved my cousin. For the past year, Roy and I had doubled dated often with Wendy and Everett, Roy's older brother. Everett's job took him out of town almost every week, so Wendy had stepped in to help Everett with his best man duties. I really owed her big time. First, she'd introduced me to my future husband, and then she'd performed all the maid of honor duties and the best man duties. She could've asked me for anything, and I would get it for her.

Dad lightly kissed my cheek. "You nervous?"

I nodded.

"You don't have to do this if you don't want. We can walk out the door, get in the car, and go home."

Turning to him, I laughed. "I want to do this but

thank you for telling me that, no matter what, you're there for me."

"In that case, I hope you'll be as happy as your mother and I have been," he said, his eyes growing misty.

"Me, too, Daddy."

As we walked down the church aisle, I saw so many of my friends and extended family. My heart swelled with pride and gratitude that so many people had given up their Saturday evening to attend my wedding.

My gaze swept the front of church, expecting to see Roy staring at me, but he wasn't. He was looking across the room. As I looked at him, his head turned toward me and he smiled, but then he looked across the room again. What had his attention? With everyone standing for my entrance I couldn't twist my head around and try to find what he was looking at. And even if I could, I'd never be able to see around all the heads in the crowd. There had to be at least five hundred people packed into the Greater Dallas Methodist Church, which wasn't surprising given that a McCool was marrying a Livingston. Either name alone would provide a draw, but both names together were too much for society to ignore.

Roy finally looked at me and smiled. I pasted on a smile as Dad and I stopped near him. My cheeks quivered from the smiling. The pastor started his spiel about marriage, and when he came to the part about who gives this woman to be with this man, my dad spoke.

He was supposed to say, "Her mother and I do," but he didn't. Instead he said, "My daughter is a mature woman. She does not need me nor her mother to give her away. She makes her own decisions, and we stand with her. Therefore, her mother and I welcome the man she has chosen as her husband into our family."

With that, he kissed my cheek and joined my mother in the front pew.

I hope my mouth didn't drop in shock. I have never been so touched by words and by his public declaration that he and Mom would welcome Roy into our family. They'd never been completely in love with the idea that I was marrying Roy, but this was their way of publicly supporting my decision. My vision blurred with tears. My parents were the best.

I turned toward Wendy to hand off my bridal bouquet. She smiled and winked. I returned her smile and wink. I turned back to Roy, and we joined hands.

His hands were damp and cold. His fingers shook as he held mine. I was pleasantly surprised and secretly pleased that he was as nervous as I was.

I'd been with Roy for over a year, and he wasn't an emotional person. In fact, there had never been passionate expressions of love and need from him. But he'd explained that once he'd hit thirty, he felt he'd matured beyond such childish declarations. At first, I'd been a little disappointed and hurt, until I'd remembered Michael Rockland.

Michael Rockland and I had had a passionate and crazy-in-love affair the summer after I'd graduated high school. It'd continued until Christmas of my freshman year of college. It'd been fiery and frantic, as though we'd wanted to be inside each other's skin. When the affair ended, I'd been bruised and crushed, and I'd decided that what I wanted in a life mate was calmness, patience, and reliability. Stability in a relationship would become more important than emotive outbursts and sex so hot the sheets caught fire.

And that's what I'd spent these last ten years looking for and found in Roy.

As the pastor droned on about love and honor and family, Roy's face continued to be somber, but his eyes kept shifting around as though he were looking past me. Abruptly, he dropped my hands and stepped back. "I can't do this," he said. "I'm sorry, Mae."

Hot SEAL, Alaskan Nights
A Dallas Debutante/SEALs in Paradise Novel

From NYT and USA Today Best Selling Author comes a beach read that isn't the typical sun-drenched location. Homer, Alaska. A Navy SEAL on leave. A nurse practitioner in seclusion. A jealous ex-lover looking for redemption...or is it revenge?

Navy SEAL Levi Van der Hayden, aka Dutch, returns to his family home in Homer, AK for the three Rs...rest, relaxation and recovery. As the only SEAL injured during his team's last mission, the last thing he wants to do is show his bullet wound to friends...it's in his left gluteus maximus and he's tired of being the butt of all the jokes (his own included.)

After a violent confrontation with a controlling, narcissistic ex-lover, nurse practitioner Bailey Brown flees Texas for Alaska. A maternal grandmother still in residence provides her with the ideal sanctuary...still in the U.S. but far enough away to escape her ex's reach.

Attracted to the cute nurse from his welcome home beach party, Levi insists on showing her the real Alaska experience. When her safety is threatened, he must use all his SEAL skills to protect her and eliminate the risk, even if it means putting his own life on the line.

Levi Van der Hayden's left butt cheek was on fire. He shifted uncomfortably in the back seat of the subcompact car masquerading as their Uber ride. As soon as he moved, the stitches in his left thigh reminded him that pushing off with that leg was also mistake.

"We should try to get upgraded when we get to the airport," Compass said.

Compass, also known as Levi's best friend Rio North, was going way out of his way to help Levi get home leave, but at this moment, Levi gritted his teeth at the ridiculous suggestion.

"I don't have the money for that and you know it." Levi, aka Dutch to his SEAL team buds, knew he shouldn't be so grumpy what with all Compass was doing for him but damn it! Why did he have to be shot in the ass? The guys would never let him live it down.

He repositioned his hips so most of the weight was on his uninjured right butt cheek.

"You bring anything for the pain, Dutch?"

"Took something about an hour ago, which right now seems like last week."

The car stopped at the Departure gates of San Diego International Airport. Dutch climbed from the back seat of the way-too-tiny car with a few choice cuss words and stood on the sidewalk. Compass paid the driver and then hefted out two duffle bags. After slinging both onto his shoulders, he gestured toward the airport with his chin.

Once inside, Compass said, "Seriously Dutch, you need to upgrade. There is no way you are going to be able to stretch out and you know what the doctor said about pulling those stitches."

Levi glared at his friend and answered him with a one-finger response.

Compass grinned back him. "All joking aside, I'll pay for your upgrade. Your ass literally *needs* to be in first class." The asshole then leaned back and glanced down at Levi's ass…well actually the cheek where he'd been shot coming back from their last fucking mission.

"No, damn it, Compass, I already told you I can't afford it and I'm not accepting charity." Levi knew his friend could afford to upgrade Levi to a big, roomy, first-class seat, but he was already taking Compass way out of his way with this trip. When his friend opened his mouth to speak, Levi held up a hand to stop him. "Not even from you. I appreciate it, man, I really do, but no." Levi shook his head emphatically. "I fucking hate being such a pain in your ass, har har har."

To say Levi had been the target of his SEAL team buddies' relentless butt jokes would be an understatement. They'd been brutal in the way only people who love you can. Levi knew that. Understood that. And would have been there throwing out the butt and ass jokes if it'd been anyone else who'd gotten shot in the ass, but it wasn't. It was him and he was tired of it. He lowered himself carefully onto a bench.

Compass looked around and then back to Levi. "Okay, look, I'm going to go talk to the agent over there. I'm not spending a dime, but sometimes they let active duty get upgrades. Let me see what I can do. Okay?"

Levi followed Compass's gaze to an attractive brunette behind the Delta service counter. He chuckled. "Damn man, you could pick up a woman anywhere, couldn't you?"

Compass shrugged, but his grin said he knew exactly what Levi was talking about. "It's a God-given talent. But that's not what this is about. Give me your military ID."

Levi pulled out his card, but hesitated. Compass had more money than God, Dropping an thousand or so dollars to change a plane ticket was probably pocket change to him, but not to Levi.

Compass jerked Levi's military card out his hand with a snort. "Shit that damaged ass muscle has fucked up your reflexes."

"Fuck you, man. It's the pain meds." Levi

narrowed his eyes at his best friend. "Not a penny, Compass, not a fucking penny. Got it?"

"Loud and clear." Compass pointed to him. "Stay here and look pathetic."

Compass had only taken a few steps before Levi heard him laugh. God damn asshole.

Jesus, he hated this. Not only was he in pain, but the damn doctors had restricted him from lifting anything over twenty pounds. Twenty pounds! Like he was some fucking girl or something. He was a Navy SEAL. He could lift twenty pounds with his toes...or could before just moving his toes made the exit wound on his thigh ache.

Now that their last mission was behind them—he groaned at his own bad joke—the team had a little time off, which meant he could finally go home for a few days. However, the restrictions from the doctors meant someone had to help him with his duffle bag since it definitely weighed more than twenty pounds. He was pissed off and embarrassed by that limit to his activities. Hell, even jogging was off his activities list until the stitches healed a little more.

He'd been ordered to do medical follow-up at the Alaskan VA Health Clinic. Knowing his commander, Skipper would follow up on that, and if Levi didn't follow orders, his ass would be grass. He groan again and ordered himself to stop with the ass jokes.

Turning his attention back to the action across the lobby Levi watched Compass operate. He was too far away to hear the conversation, but he knew his friend's M.O. well. He'd smile. He'd compliment the woman.

Then he'd toss in his best friend's war wound for sympathy. Levi snorted to himself. He'd seen Compass in action too many times to count.

Compass leaned toward the Delta agent and Levi was sure the poor woman had been sucked into Compass's charismatic gravitational pull. She didn't stand a chance against a pro like Compass.

When Compass set both of their duffle bags on the scale and the airline agent tagged them, Levi was at least sure he was going home. What he didn't know was if it would be in the front of the plane or the back of the plane. If it weren't for his ass and leg, he wouldn't care where he sat, but he knew that wasn't true for his friend, who always went first-class when he could.

Compass turned from the check-in desk and started toward Levi with a broad smile he'd seen before when Compass got what he wanted.

Levi eyed him. "Why do you have a shit-eating grin on your face? What did you do?"

"I'm smiling because I'm a fucking magic man." He handed Levi a boarding pass.

Levi studied the boarding pass with first class all in capital letters. "Did you buy this?" His lips tightened into a straight line.

Compass help up his hands. "Nope. Not a penny spent. I swear on my mother's grave."

"Your mother is alive, asshole."

"Yeah, but we have a family plot and we all have real estate allotted. I swear *I* didn't spend a single dime on that ticket man. That pretty little thing over there hooked you up." He motioned over to Brittany who was busy with another customer.

"Sir, are you ready?"

Levi's gaze fell on an attendant pushing a wheelchair. "What the fuck?"